DAY *One*

ISBN: 9798642789872

#AloneTogether

Dedicated to everyone! We're all in this together. ♥

Day 1

March 27, 2020

I open my fridge for the fifth time today. I don't even know why. I'm not hungry, just bored. If I don't get my boredom eating under control, I'll gain weight during all of this, and also my food storage is starting to dwindle.

I'm on day ten of a shelter-in-place mandate from the Governor of California. There are only a few cases in my small town of the dreaded coronavirus, but just a few miles up the road, a few hundred have been reported, so they've put us all on lockdown to stop the spread.

I knew it was coming. As a sixth-grade teacher, I knew shit was about to go down when they canceled school for two weeks before the shelter in place was even ordered. Canceling schools is a big deal, so when that surprising announcement came, I prepared for more.

I stopped by the supermarket before I went home, grabbed everything I needed for two weeks, and planned on enjoying the time off by relaxing and doing whatever I wanted.

Yeah, that lasted all of about three days before I was

Day One

bored out of my mind. By Tuesday, I was starting to twid-dle my thumbs. Now that it is Friday, I'm itching to go out, but I can't. Everywhere is closed, and when you live alone, you really start to realize how much you rely on outside interaction to keep you going.

My parents who live a few hours away have been checking in with me, and for the first time, I've felt it's a good thing they divorced after I graduated high school because, now, I get two phone calls instead of one to keep me entertained.

That's how sad my days have become.

I've tried to stay in touch with my friends, but since all of their children are home now, they're losing their minds, and they can't talk on the phone without having to yell at their kids, or it's so loud that they can barely hear me, which ends in them feeling frustrated and having to hang up the phone. I've gotten joking texts saying, *Send wine*, from more people than I can count.

I decide to put mind over matter and shut the refriger-ator door.

I. Am. Not. Hungry. I repeat in my mind.

Picking up my phone, I sigh as I scroll through Face-book for the tenth time today, seeing if anything new has been posted, when my notification dings with a message from Tinder.

I reactivated Tinder over the weekend after taking a hiatus. I figured my messages would be going crazy right now with everyone at home bored but that's not the case. It's like guys know they can't get laid right now, so they're not even putting in the effort. When New York City sent out a message that went so viral even I saw it here in Cali-fornia saying, *You are your safest sex partner*, I knew things were getting real.

I open the app and see I have a message from a guy named Drew. It's been a while since I swiped right, so I click on his profile to see if I remember ever seeing this guy.

He only has one picture available for me to view. He's wearing a baseball cap and a smile. It's cut close and I can't see his entire body, but he's pretty good-looking, so I snoop some more to read:

DREW, 27
TEN MILES AWAY
JUST A GUY FOLLOWING HIS DREAM.

The space allows for a paragraph, so him having only one sentence intrigues me, mainly because I like the sentiment. I like someone who has goals and isn't afraid to put them out there for all to see.

Since I'm bored, I decide, *Why not?* I open the message to see what he said.

Drew: Hey there. Are you bored like me?

I laugh out loud because he truly has no idea just how bored I am. I decide to play with him.

Me: I was actually just about to find a cure for cancer, but boo, I got interrupted by your message, and now, the entire thought is gone. Oh well. On to the next.

Drew: Nice to know I'll go down in history as the guy who got caught up by a pretty girl and ruined all of humanity because of it.

Me: Pretty, you say? Do tell …

I'm shocked when I hit Send. I must be totally losing my mind because that is not something I'd normally say to a guy.

Day One

Drew: From what I saw, I'd say yes. Please
don't tell me those are pictures you found online to pose as someone else …

I decide to just go for it, showing him what's really going on over here. I hold up my phone and take a picture in
all my quarantined glory. Before I think twice, I hit Send.

Me: Don't judge. I haven't left the house in
days, so messy bun it is.

When he returns the favor by sending me a picture of
him lounging on his couch, I pause to take in the photo.
His profile one was cute, but it's nothing compared to the
sexy guy who's now gracing my screen, especially because
he didn't take the time to find better lighting or pose in a
douchey way.

His photo comes off as laid-back, and that's the kind of
guy I want. I'm sick of men who think they're God's gift to
women. This guy has a cocky way about him but in a sexy
way, not an eye-roll way.

He has a ball cap on that looks old and worn, and I can
tell the lounge pants he's wearing hug him in all the right
places because, yeah, he showed me all the goods.

Fully clothed, that is.

I smile as I text.

Me: I call bullshit. Send me another photo
that proves it's you by doing something silly.

Being a sixth-grade teacher, I swear I'm only slightly
above their maturity level, and I love when I get to play
with people like this. Life's too short to be so serious.

A picture of him with wide eyes while he's blowing out
his cheeks as big as possible appears on my screen within
seconds. I laugh out loud at how ridiculous he looks but
also at how playful he is.

Drew: I would have pulled my ears out, too, but I needed to hold my phone to take the photo.

Me: Fine. I believe it's you. ;-)

Drew: Oh no, you don't get off that easy. Your turn. Show me your silly face.

I raise one eyebrow, cross my eyes, stick my tongue out to the side while tilting my head to the right, and snap a photo, hitting Send without even looking at it. When it appears on the screen, I slap my hand to my forehead. *I can't believe I just sent that!*

Drew: Well, Sharee, it's nice to meet you. What have you been doing during this fine time on lockdown?

Me: Sigh … nothing. You've been the most exciting thing to happen to me in over a week.

I hit Send and then shake my head at how that sounded, so I go on.

Me: Yikes. That sounded so lame. I swear I'm not that lame. I just live alone, and I never realized how bad that sucked until I couldn't leave my house.

Drew: I hear you. I've been gone, and now, I'm back home and not sure what to do.

Me: Where were you?

Day One

Drew: A little bit of everywhere.

Me: For work?

Drew: Yeah. How about you? What do you do for a living?

Drew: Wow. Now, I sound lame. When did we get old enough to ask someone that?

Me: Right?! But I get it. I'm a sixth-grade teacher.

Drew: So, you're off for a while then?

Me: Yep. At least I'm still getting paid. How about you? Are you working right now or no?

Drew: I'm off but still getting paid. I just signed on right before all this went down, so I got lucky. I know a few guys who didn't, and they're scrambling right now. Kinda sucks, you know?

Me: Yeah, everyone's in the same boat, so hopefully, things will work out. What do you do?

Drew: I'm following my dreams for as long as I can.

Me: Yeah, your profile said that.

Drew: So, you checked me out before responding?

Me: Duh, of course I did. Though you didn't give me much to go by. I haven't swiped right in months so I don't remember you, to be honest.

Drew: I'm not sure if that's a good thing or bad thing. But I haven't been on the app in months, so it might have been a long time ago, and you just showed up in my choices.

Me: Choices, huh? You got a lot of choices? Is that why you haven't been on the app? Are you newly single?

Drew: I meant, lovely options. Does that sound better? And no, just too busy. I haven't dated in a while.

Me: So, you travel and are too busy … sounds like you're looking for a healthy relationship. You do realize we're quarantined, so booty calls are out of the picture, right?

Drew: Damn, straight to booty calls. I thought that was another app?

Me: Oh, believe me, it's on this app too.

Drew: Is that why you're on it?

Day One

Me: Oh God. I totally came off that way, didn't I? But no. I'm not your booty call girl, so if that's what you're looking for, you can move right along.

Drew: Nah. I'm good right here. Tell me more about yourself.

Me: Well, I already told you, I'm a teacher. I love science so though I teach all subjects every day, if I were teaching today, we would be dissecting a squid.

Drew: Would you have had the kids write with the ink?

Me: OMG, yes! It's the coolest ever. What would you be doing today if you weren't stuck at home?

Drew: I'd have to check my schedule to see where I would have been. But now, I'm stuck at home with no sports to watch.

Me: Sports fan, huh? What's your favorite?

Drew: Baseball. Yesterday would have been opening day. Please tell me you like baseball, or this is never going to work. ;-)

Me: You're in luck! Or I'm in luck. Not sure yet. But, yes, I love baseball. I just happen to have the best player in town as my nephew. He plays for the Titans.

Drew: Yeah? I played for them back in the day.

Me: How cool! They're supposed to go to Cooperstown in June, but with all of this going on, their trip is up in the air, and my sister is stressing out. Going is like a dream to them.

Drew: Yeah, I'd be upset, too, if I didn't get to go. Some of my best memories were from there.

I start to type him more questions about the trip, but he sends another text before I can.

Drew: Hey, I hate to cut this short, but my roommates just got home, and I have to help them with something. I'd love to chat with you some more. Can we pick up where we left off tomorrow?

Me: I'll be here, stuck at home.

Drew: It's a date. Chat then.

I close the app and bring my phone to my chest with a big smile on my face. *Maybe this quarantine won't be so bad after all.*

Day 2

March 28

I have to admit, I'm stupidly excited when I hear the chime of my Tinder message—and, yes, I changed the tone, so I would know it was from Tinder and not a normal text message.

> Drew: I saw a meme on Facebook that made me think of you.

Below the text is a pink box that says, *It's only the first week of school, and I'm already trying to get this kid transferred out of my class.*

I laugh out loud. I've seen so many parents vent about how frustrated they are with having to homeschool their kids, but I haven't seen that one yet. I text back.

> Me: Been there. LOL! I feel bad for these parents. They need to understand that their kids don't act that way in school. It's the kid's job to test the limits of their parents. They have a way harder job now than I do on any normal day.

I hit Send and then remember a few memes I saw my sister post today. I go to her Instagram account and screenshot them.

Me: This reminded me of you today.

The first picture is of a baseball with text over it, saying, *Would y'all please keep your asses at home? I want baseball back.*

Drew: Yes!!! Please, for the love of everything holy, yes!

I smile and then send the next picture of a baseball that has the face of Wilson from the movie *Cast Away*.

Drew: Ha! That's awesome! I saw someone actually gave Tom Hanks a Wilson volleyball with that face on it while he was in quarantine recently.

Drew: So, you thought about me twice today?

A cheesy grin comes across my face as I curl up into my couch.

Me: Maybe more … but by your logic, does that mean you only thought about me once today?

My phone dings with five different memes, all about parents having to teach and having a hard time doing so.

I cover my mouth, laughing out loud at all of them, but I'm also overly excited about how many he screenshot. When I look closer, I notice he didn't take the time to crop the image, so I see that each one is hours apart from the other, starting last night.

Day One

Me: Those are awesome! But maybe even more awesome is that you took the time to share them with me.

Drew: I think you'll be in the most appreciated profession when all of this is over.

I smile, hoping that's true. Then, I think ...

Me: Do you have kids? Just curious. Not a big deal if you do.

Drew: Nope. No kids here. At least, not that I know of.

My eyes open wide in shock.

Drew: Yeah, that was a lame attempt at a joke.

I grin.

Me: You're forgiven. ;-) What else did you do today?

Drew: I had an idea ... well, wishful thinking is more like it.

A picture comes across the screen of him wearing a San Francisco Giants jersey. Today, he doesn't have on a hat, and I can see his hair is a dirty-blond with hints of brown woven in. Most girls would kill for his color, and I can only assume, or hope, it's natural.

His eyes light up in the photo, showing off their hazel color, and it doesn't seem like he shaved today, as his five o'clock shadow is well past midnight.

Drew: I'm hoping it's like the *Field of Dreams* movie. "If you build it, they will come." So, I figured if I wore it, it will come … I can dream at least.

Me: You're too cute. But, yeah, I don't think it works that way.

Drew: What about you? What have you been up to?

Me: A whole bunch of nothing. Normally, on Saturdays, I go to yoga in the morning and then spend time with my sister and my nephews. I tried to take a yoga class they offered online, but it wasn't the same. Yoga and carpet don't really mix.

Drew: Yoga, huh? Are you super flexible?

Me: Get your mind out of the gutter.

Drew: ;-)

Drew: But in all seriousness, people have said I should try yoga to help build my strength and flexibility. Who knows? Maybe when all of this is over, I'll take a class with you.

Me: I'd like that—as long as you don't embarrass me. You're not one of those guys who can't bend over for shit and will fall all over the place, are you?

Day One

Drew: Jeez, thanks for the vote of confidence. But no need to worry; I stretch before and after I work out, just like the doctor orders.

Me: OK. Then, I'll keep you posted when this is over.

Drew: How long do you think that will be?

Me: Our school was pushed back to May 1st yesterday. Hoping we return sooner than that, but no one really knows. They asked me to work on my distance learning, so I've been making YouTube videos to share with my students.

Drew: You have to send me the link.

Me: No way in hell.

Drew: Oh, come on. Let me hear your voice.

Me: The only one I've made so far is about King Tut and Egypt. It's a rap video that I sang along to.

Drew: Now, I NEED to see the video. Please. You can't tease me with rapping about King Tut and not share.

Me: OMG! No way!

Drew: Hmm … I just figured out how I'm going to spend my day tomorrow …

Me: How?

Drew: Finding out if I know anyone in your class, so I can get them to send me the link. It's a small town, you know. I'm sure I can find one person …

Me: You don't even know where I teach.

Drew: True. But I'm guessing there are not many sixth-grade teachers between the four elementary schools in town. I know a lot of people here. I have connections …

Me: If you know a lot of people, then how come I'm just meeting you?

Drew: Like I said, I've been gone for a while. But I'm back, hopefully for good now.

Drew: Am I going to have to play detective or …

I giggle at the notion of him searching for who I am and then pause when I think about how he'll tell said people how we met. I don't really want fellow teachers or my principal knowing I'm on Tinder, so I give in.

Me: Fine. Here.

I send him the link and close my eyes in horror of what he's about to see. The video is ten minutes long, and when five minutes go by, my heart starts to race. There is zero reason for him to watch the entire thing. I rap in the first two minutes, and then go over lesson plans and how the next week will work.

Seven minutes go by.

Ten minutes.

Twelve minutes!

I inhale, too embarrassed to say anything. He probably saw that and said, *Yeah, this girl is crazy*, before shutting off his phone. Like I said, I'm just barely above my students' maturity level, and that video proves it. I even went as far as getting dressed up in an Egyptian toga.

Many students have told me that I'm their favorite teacher, but they're eleven years old. I'm sure some adults think I never grew up.

After twenty minutes, I give up. I throw my phone across the cushion and get up to pour myself a big glass of wine.

Before I make it to the couch, I hear the distinctive ding of my Tinder account. Almost spilling my wine, I rush over to the phone and swipe it on. To my surprise, it's a video.

I click it and instantly laugh out loud at the sight of Drew wrapped in a sheet, singing his own rap. From what I can tell, it was shot with his phone resting on a dresser that's about waist high. He has his shirt off, and his arms shine through the cream-colored fabric wrapped around him. They're lean and tone with defined muscles, and his chest is ... flawless.

His rap is only six lines long, but I'm dying, laughing the entire time. He's playing the role really well, and when he leans down to turn off the camera, he makes a little face, playfully sticking his tongue out before clicking the video off.

I watch it over and over again, loving it more and more each time.

Me: I'm SO showing this to my students.

Drew: Don't you dare. That was fun though.

Me. That was awesome. I give you an A!

Drew: Wow! Thanks, Teach.

Drew: That video was pretty cool though. I wish I'd had a teacher like you. School was never really my thing. I only had good grades so I could play sports.

Me: Hey, whatever motivates you, take it! I have a few students like you in my class. Doing stuff like this makes them realize that learning can be fun.

Drew: I would have had such a crush on you in elementary school.

Me: Ha! Don't even talk like that. I can't, just … no …

Drew: LOL! I said ME, not your students.

Me: Let's talk about now instead. Would you say you have a crush on me now?

Drew: Absolutely. And after that video… <3

My face blushes when I send him a GIF of a girl seductively raising her eyebrows.

Day One

A few minutes pass, and I'm wondering if our conversation is over until he comes back with:

Drew: So, yeah, I just had to explain to one of my roommates why I was wearing my sheet as a toga. Thanks a lot for that one.

I laugh out loud.

Me: Sorry! What did they say?

Drew: That I must be pretty smitten with a girl to do that.

Me: Smitten?

Drew: Yeah, smitten. Do people even use that word anymore?

Me: Obviously, your roommate does.

Drew: OK, well, now that I'm fully embarrassed in my own home, I'll let you go. How about I give you an actual call tomorrow?

Me: Sure. Call 867-5309.

Drew: Does that mean for a good-time call, or are you telling me, after that video, you'll never give me your real number and you'd rather never talk to me again?

Me: Just playing with you.

I give him my real number, smiling so big that my cheeks hurt.

Drew: I'll talk to you tomorrow, Sharee.

Me: OK, Drew.

I close my app and let out a little squeal. *This could definitely be something!*

Day 3

March 29

My phone rings with a 718 area code and *New York* displayed underneath it. Normally, I don't answer these types of calls, but boredom has officially taken over, and maybe I can mess with a salesperson enough to get them to talk to me. At this point, I just want human interaction, and I'll take it anywhere I can get it.

"Hello?" I say.

"Hey, it's Drew." A breathy male voice comes across my line, making my body tingle.

"Hey," I say, a little too excited. I try to bring it down a notch as I curl my body on my couch. "How come your number says New York?"

"Yeah, I lived there a while back, just never changed it. What are you up to?"

"Livin' the dream, watching the rain outside and contemplating my next move in life."

"Are you thinking big things are to come?"

" 'Big mistake! Big! HUGE,' " I drawl out. " 'I have to go shopping now…' " I let my voice trail off.

"So, you're an eighties movie buff too? Do you know anything from our generation?" he says with a slight laugh.

I return the sound. "Yeah, I just watched the *Behind the Scenes* show from *Pretty Woman*, so it's on my mind. Next is *The Breakfast Club*, and they even have one for the show *The Facts of Life*, so I have my lineup for tonight all planned out. I know you're jealous."

"You do know I have cable, so I can watch it too, right?"

"Yeah, but I'm sure you have way better things to do with your time."

"Not really, but you'll have to fill me in on what *The Facts of Life* is. I don't remember that one."

I sigh. "It was a television show from the eighties. I have an older sister; that's the only way I know about it. So, how about you? What's your day been like?"

"First, I went for a run in the rain. That was fun. Came home soaked and took a hot shower."

"Okay, hold that thought. Getting visual ..." I pause. "Yep, got it. Go on."

His laugh is deep and throaty. I close my eyes and let it soak in, especially with that visual still running through my head.

"Since then, I've been trying to stay busy. I had old boxes to go through that had been sitting in my room for the past few years, so I figured it was time."

"Ah, trip down memory lane. Did you find anything good?"

"Besides old trophies, yearbooks, and my graduation cap, not really."

"Let me guess. You were voted Best Smile in high school."

His laugh graces me again. "Thank you, but no. I was voted Most Athletic though."

I yawn loudly into the phone, teasing him.

"That bores you?" he asks with a chuckle.

"Athlete schmathlete. I'm a science nerd, remember?"

"If I say I was also a 4.0 student, too, would that turn you on?"

"Oh, talk dirty to me, baby. How many AP classes did you take?" Thankfully, he knows I'm kidding. "So, how much stuff did you actually throw away?"

"None of it." He laughs. "It was pretty cool to see what my mom had kept over the years for me. She had every jersey and every hat from the different Little League teams I played on, as well as all the tryouts performance charts I did over the years."

"Did you play in college too?"

He pauses for a brief moment and then says, "Um, yeah."

"Where'd you go?"

"Vanderbilt," he says with a nonchalance that makes my eyes bulge.

"Seriously?" I ask, shocked. "How come you left that out?"

A sharp laugh escapes his lips. "Is that how you date nowadays? *Hi, I'm Drew. I have a degree from Vanderbilt, so I'm not a schlep. Do you want to get to know me?*"

I giggle into the phone. "Well, yeah. It wouldn't hurt. You'd be surprised how many losers are out there."

"Is that why you're still single? Nothing but losers?"

"You have no idea how many guys still live with their parents." There's an awkward pause, so I continue, "Did you know most relationships start at work? When you're surrounded by eleven-year-olds and ninety percent of your coworkers are women, it makes it kind of difficult to meet people."

"So, that's why you're on Tinder?" he asks.

"To be honest, my sister created my account. She's dying for nieces or nephews. Since she's older, she's out of the baby stage and says it's my turn. Oh my God"—I panic—"I'm sorry. I know that's like dating 101—to not talk about wanting babies." I smack my forehead. "I swear I'm not like Marisa Tomei, stomping my foot while whining, 'My biological clock is ticking like this,' " I say in my best accent to match hers from the movie *My Cousin Vinny*.

"Hey, I think that's from the nineties, right? Look at you, moving up in the decades," he teases.

"*Pretty Woman* was actually released in 1990, so give me a little credit on that one, but challenge accepted. I'll try to think of one from the 2000s now."

"Can't wait to hear what you come up with," he says just as I hear a knock in the background.

"Sweetheart, would you mind running out to get the food we ordered?" an older female voice says.

My eyes open wide as I sit up on my couch. *Sweetheart? Who is that asking him to go get something?*

I can tell he's muffled the phone by the loud swooshing sound coming through on my end. He's responding, but I can't hear what he says. When he comes back, the line is silent, and I give him all the time he needs to explain who that was.

"So ..." He laughs nervously. "Why do I feel like I'm back in high school and I was just caught talking to a girl?"

"Um, because it sounds like you were. Do you live with your parents still?"

"No. Yes. I mean—"

"*You mean*?" I pause. "Please tell me it's not what I think."

"It isn't, I promise."

I can hear the panic in his voice, and it's almost cute. He's nervous, and I take that as a good sign.

He continues, "Yes, I'm staying with my parents right now but only because my place isn't ready yet. I've only been here for a few weeks. I was supposed to move on April first, but with everything going on, that date's been pushed back."

Day One

"Hmm," I tease him. "Are you sure you're not like the other losers I've met?" Hopefully, he can hear the playfulness in my voice.

He sighs. "Okay, you caught me. I'm the biggest loser out there, and really, I'm in my parents' basement right now, buried in old comic books and covered in Cheetos cheese dust."

Now, it's my turn to laugh out loud. "I knew it!"

He lets out a breathy laugh and then says, "It actually couldn't have been better timing. My mom's a cancer survivor, but it's only been a few years since she's been in remission, so my parents are staying home. I've been running all of their errands for them, so my dad doesn't have to worry about possibly infecting her. I do my best to not touch things while I'm out, and then I keep my distance from them—well, as much as I can while living in their house."

"That's pretty cool. So, where did you move from?"

"Chicago."

"You have a New York number but used to live in Chicago?"

"Yeah, I told you, I travel a lot, but I'll call here home now—at least for a little while."

"If you lived in Chicago, how did I swipe right on you a few months ago?"

"I was home for a while over the holidays. It was probably then. I might or might not have opened the app a few times when I was here."

"Hmm, the truth comes out." I chuckle.

"Guilty as charged. Nothing came from it though."

"What, no late-night hook-ups that you snuck into your parents' home after they went to bed?"

He laughs. "Um, yeah, that's a big no."

"Wait, so the roommate you mentioned yesterday, who walked in on you when you were dressed in a toga, was your mom?"

"Yes!" he says, his voice raising an octave. "That took some explaining, thanks to you."

"Makes sense now. Of course a mom would say *smitten*."

"Yes, she did. Look, I hate to cut this short, but as you heard, I have to go fetch them some food."

My eyes light up in excitement. " 'That is so fetch!' " I say with a Valley Girl tone. " 'Gretchen, stop trying to make fetch happen! It's not going to happen!' "

"You did it!" He laughs. "And don't ask me how I know that movie."

"Oh, I'm going to ask; don't you worry." I giggle.

"Talk to you tomorrow?"

"You got it. Night, Drew."

"Bye, Sharee."

The way he says my name is so sexy that I swear I feel my heart swoon. I love having this little time in my day to look forward to, and he's not disappointing me at all.

Day 4

March 30

I finally did it! I actually did my hair today and put on makeup. I had been afraid my hair would be permanently kinked with how long I'd been throwing it up in a messy bun right out of the shower.

I wish I could say it's because I have something special to do or somewhere to go, but no. I'm having a Zoom meeting with my students, and though I might have their same maturity level, I always try to look as professional as possible when I teach my class.

I sent out the link to the Zoom meeting this morning, and I'm praying some students show up. Most of my class have their own cell phones, so I made sure to give instructions on how to download the app, so they can talk to me on their devices.

As I sit at my kitchen counter, after making sure everything in the background is appropriate for my class to see, I log on.

My face fills the entire screen, and I flinch at the size of my head, quickly covering my face. With a laugh, I peek behind my hands to ease myself into the view of the camera, which is pointed up at me in an unflattering way.

Next time, I for sure need to work on the angle of this thing as well as the lighting.

One after another, multiple boxes pop up on my screen, showing the students I miss so much. Everyone talks over one another, and the expressions on their faces are priceless when they see their friends they haven't been around for almost two weeks.

I let them all take it in and enjoy the moment. After all, this is probably the most exciting thing that's happened to them as well. It's obvious that multiple conversations are going at once, and I try to figure out who is actually talking to who.

After a few minutes, I speak up and try to get their attention, "Hey, everyone."

They all quiet down.

"How are you all doing?"

I see some shrugs and some nods, and a few kids actually answer by saying, "All right."

"How about you, Ms. Witzel?" Timmy asks.

I give the same response, "I'm all right. Staying inside, like I hope you all are doing as well." I see a few kids nod before I continue, "But to be totally honest ... I'm so bored!"

The kids all laugh and agree. "Yes!" I hear a collective response.

We discuss the distance-learning assignments I assigned through Google Classroom and what this week should look like.

The whole thing amazes me. Thanks to technology, we're making this work. If this had happened when I was their age, none of this would have been possible. Shoot, I didn't even know Zoom existed until last week, and now, it's all over the place! I've had to talk to a few parents just to walk them through how to log on to Google Classroom, as even that is over their heads.

"I saw something online today that I really want you guys to consider," I say. "And no, it's not an assignment, nor will you actually be turning this in. I want you to do this because *you* want to and nothing more."

A few kids roll their eyes, and I can tell they've checked out, so I try to bring them back in.

"How many of you have grandparents who fought in the Vietnam War?"

A few raise their hands.

"Okay, what about September 11? Do you know anyone who was personally affected by the attacks on the World Trade Center?"

Only one raises her hand. Since we're in California, I'm not too surprised on this one.

"Then, let's think about your great-grandparents. Did anyone fight in World War II or the Korean War?"

A few more raise their hands.

"Now, imagine if you could read their journal from back then. My dad fought in the Vietnam War, and I've had the opportunity to read every letter he sent home to my grandparents during that time. By just reading his letters, I learned way more about that period in history than I ever could have in any textbook. It was fascinating because he was actually living in the fields of an unknown area during a very uncertain time in our history."

"But what does that have to do with what's going on now? We're not at war," Nick asks.

"No, we aren't, but I absolutely guarantee you that your grandchildren will be reading about today, the pandemic of 2020, in their history books. This is affecting the entire world! I hope you realize that we haven't dealt with anything like this since 1918 with the Spanish flu. So, how cool would it be if they got to read your journal during this time?"

Some shrug as others take it seriously.

"That would be pretty cool," Angeline says.

"If you're interested, I encourage you to write down what your day is like. What your thoughts and fears are. Just remember, your grandchildren might want to read it someday, so watch what you say," I tease.

Once all the important stuff is out of the way, I give each student a few minutes to talk about what they're doing at home and to share anything they want.

I listen as they tell me about shows they're watching and things they're doing to stay busy.

When I get to Nick, he's eager to ask me, "Ms. Witzel, do you know Andrew Miller?"

I think about the name Andrew and shake my head. "It doesn't ring a bell. Why?"

He frowns. "He's the new guy they just signed to the San Francisco Giants. He made a YouTube video, going over tips for kids on how to stay in shape for baseball at home and how to keep practicing when they have no one to practice with. In the video, he said he got the idea from a teacher who made a video of a rapping King Tut, so I thought that was you. I know his parents live here and—"

My eyes widen, and my face flushes when what he said sinks in. Then, the name Andrew—*Drew*—clicks in my head.

Oh. My. God.

"Did you say San Francisco Giants? As in the San Francisco Giants baseball team?"

Memories of him wearing a jersey the other day and making a joke by tying it to the movie *Field of Dreams* flash through my mind.

Was that his *actual jersey?*

"Yeah," Nick says. "I can't believe there are other teachers who would rap about King Tut because, come on, Ms. Witzel, that was a little"—he makes the international sign for crazy by circling his ear with his finger—"cuckoo."

"No, it wasn't," a few kids chime in to defend me.

I laugh. "Well, I'm sorry you didn't like my very cool song, but I'll look into this other teacher who's rapping to my tunes." I make a fake angry face while I'm internally freaking out.

We end our Zoom, and I'm quick to do an internet search for this Andrew Miller guy. Multiple results pop up, and I read all about the golden boy who shone during spring training and was finally making his way up to the major leagues after being in the minors for five years.

I click on a photo, and on my screen is the face of the guy I've come to know as Drew.

I've thought about calling him all day, but I still haven't. What would I say? *Hey, are you the baseball player who just signed a nine-million-dollar contract?*

Ugh!

All I can think about is, *Why didn't he tell me?*

But then, when I think back to our conversations, he was stating it without actually saying it. He talked about moving a lot, how he'd just signed on—shit, he even showed me a picture of himself in *his* jersey! *How was I supposed to know that was* his *actual jersey with* his *name written across the back instead of Posey or Crawford?*

Does he assume I know who he is? Is he one of those guys who has this huge ego and thinks that everyone should automatically recognize him?

I'm so confused.

And this is why I've fought all day not to call him, instead waiting to see if he calls me.

When my phone rings at nine o'clock that night, I've

gone through all the emotions, and really, I'm over it, so I answer the phone call, making sure he knows that I know.

"Why didn't you tell me?" I say instead of the normal hello.

I can hear his nervous laugh over the line and the fact that he is totally caught off guard when he replies, "Uh, tell you what?"

"Who you are. I mean, who you *really* are." The line is silent. "Did you assume I already knew?"

"No."

With how fast he responded, I believe him. I calm down slightly, knowing I'm being a little overdramatic. "Then, why didn't you tell me?"

He lets out a breath. "Do you know how hard it is to meet someone—I mean, genuinely meet someone—when they know you're a baseball player?"

I sigh. "Okay, go on."

"I take it, you Googled me."

A hard laugh escapes my lips. "Uh, yeah, I totally did."

"So, imagine if everyone knew your net worth. Like, overnight, you went from making four hundred dollars a week to signing a contract worth millions of dollars."

"Yeah, okay."

"You'd be surprised at how many people have come out of the woodwork to be my friend again. Especially girls." He sighs. "The past few months have been a whirlwind. They all knew it was coming. News stations were covering me left and right. It's a little overwhelming is all."

My shoulders slump, and I feel bad for questioning him or for even being mad at him for not telling me.

"I wanted to see if I could get to know someone for me, not because of the contract I signed."

"I'm sorry. I understand now."

"Do you forgive me?" he asks in his sweet voice.

"It's more like, do you forgive me? I shouldn't have

asked you like that. It's just that one of my students saw your video—"

He laughs out loud. "So, they mentioned I got the idea from yours?"

"Yes!" I whine out. "He asked if I knew you, but he called you Andrew, so I was thrown off until he mentioned the video. Why does your profile say Drew?"

"Is it bad that I was purposely trying to pull away from Andrew, the new San Francisco Giants first baseman, and just be Drew, the guy still chasing after his dreams?"

I grin from ear to ear. "So, what do you prefer to be called?"

"Honestly, my friends call me Drew, but Andrew is okay too."

"Then, are we friends?" I ask coyly.

"I'm hoping we're more than friends."

Yes. Me too, Drew. Me too.

Day 5

Last night, Drew and I stayed on the phone until one in the morning. We talked about everything yet nothing at all. I felt like I was a teenager again, sneaking around to hide from my parents and talking to the boy I liked from school.

Thank God I don't have to get ready for work today, or I would be a mess. Hmm. This is the first time I've thought it is a good thing that I'm stuck at home.

I ventured out to get groceries this morning, and holy hell, the line to get into Costco was insane. I guess it's because they're limiting the amount of people in the stores rather than having too many people all together, but all I can say is, wow!

After scrubbing my hands with soap I have outside so I can clean myself of any germs with the hose and not risk bringing anything into my house, I grab my groceries and place them on the counter.

Memories of the employee loading my stuff into my cart crosses my mind, and I mentally panic. Grabbing a Clorox wipe, I clean off every box and can before putting them on my shelves. A little much? Probably, but I do not want to get this.

Once everything is put away, I hop in the shower, questioning for a second if I should burn the clothes I had on but deciding I shouldn't be that much of a worrywart about it. My county only has forty-nine cases, so yes, I should be cautious, but I'm not absolutely freaking out—yet.

If I were in New York City, I would be losing my ever-loving mind, never leaving the house and foraging for food like a squirrel in my backyard.

Wait, does New York even have squirrels like we do here? I shake my head. *Of course they do, just maybe not where I could afford to live in the concrete jungle.*

I'd be screwed.

After my shower and pulling my hair up into my hairdo of the pandemic—a messy bun—I head downstairs to search through all the stuff I just bought, being thankful I'm not a squirrel.

When my phone goes off, I don't even look to see who it is when I answer, saying, "Hello?" after I take a big bite of a banana.

"Did I catch you at a bad time?" Drew says, all drawn out and slow.

I chew faster, saying, "Hold on," and then swallow. "Sorry, I took a bite of a banana right as you called."

"Thinking of me, were you?" He laughs.

"I said bite, not lick. I really hope you're not into the whole biting thing because that might be a little out of my forte."

I'm rewarded with my favorite thing about him. His throaty laugh.

"Hey, do you have plans tonight?" he asks, and I instantly laugh out loud.

"Well, first, I am going to march in the women's rights

parade, and then I'm going to go see my favorite band tonight. I'm so excited! There's going to be thousands of people and mosh pits and all these crowds everywhere. I'd offer for you to come, but"—I sigh—"sorry, it's sold out."

"Damn, and I really wanted to be in a mosh pit tonight. I hear that's the absolute best way to get this virus. Especially if the people next to you are screaming and singing along, spit flying out of their mouths. That, mixed with their sweat while literally being on top of each other, sounds like my dream night."

I can't stop my giggling. I love that he plays along with my sarcastic ways.

"But seriously, I'd like to take you on a date, quarantine-style," he says.

"Quarantine-style? Why does that sound like I should be concerned?"

"I have an idea, but ..." he drawls out his last word.

"There's always a *but*," I tease. "If it's too good to be true ..." I trail off.

"I need your address. I promise I won't come in or even come close to you. I just ... well, it's a surprise."

"So, let's see ... you want to take me on a quarantine date that contains a surprise and butts ..." See, I told you, I have the maturity level of my students.

"Okay, maybe not butts. We'll save that for later."

I sigh dramatically. "Fine. You just took the best part out, but I guess it will do."

I give him my address, and we agree to six o'clock, though I have no idea what I just agreed to.

Six o'clock rolls around, and I nervously tap my fingers on my counter, wondering what this date will look like.

Day One

The Ring app activates, and when I open it up, I see Drew walking up to my porch. He has something in his hand, but for the life of me, I can't figure out what it is. I wait for him to ring the doorbell, so I don't come off too eager, but he doesn't.

Instead, he places whatever he's holding down and walks away. I stare into my phone, moving closer to it to see what's going on as he walks down the steps and to his car, which appears to still be running.

He places his hands in his pockets, and the video hits its time limit and shuts off.

Damn video!

I run to my front door and look out the peephole. He doesn't move but just stands there, like he's waiting for something.

Did he see my Ring? Is he expecting me to come to the door without him actually knocking?

I bite my lip in thought, but before I can make a decision, I see another car come to the driveway. The sign on top of the car shows a local Italian place.

Drew talks to the guy, and I watch as he hands Drew one of the packages out of his bag. Drew grabs something out of his car, hands it to the guy, and then points to the door, saying something else. The guy nods, taking the other part of the delivery to me.

"Should I knock?" I hear the guy ask from behind the door.

I laugh as I hear Drew yell, "Yeah. I'm sure she's sitting there, watching us right now through her Ring."

I stand up straight, holding my head high.

Ah, not this girl. Little does he know that I'm going old school and spying on him through the peephole and not all high-tech with the Ring.

The guy knocks, and I stand still for a few seconds before stomping my feet as if I were walking to the door.

When I open it, I give my most surprised face to see him standing there and then try to act even more surprised when I see Drew off in the distance.

I wave at him and then ask, "What's this?" I take the food from the guy.

He walks off and turns to Drew. "Hey, good luck, man."

Drew smirks and then looks back to me. "I bought you dinner. That's the first part of our date."

The smile on my face starts to hurt my cheeks; it's so big.

"What's in the bag?" I ask, motioning to the item Drew gave the delivery boy.

"That's for later. Oh, and I brought you something else too."

He points to the ground, and I instantly crack up laughing.

Sitting at my feet is what looks like plastic wrap that would go around flowers, but instead, it's wrapped around toilet paper, which has been arranged to resemble flowers.

I look up at him. "You did not!"

He grins and shrugs. "I figured that was more appropriate nowadays than actual flowers."

"So, you did mean to include butts!" I yell.

His head drops to his chest, and I can see his shoulders bouncing with laughter. "Okay, fine, I did. Go get set up, and I'll call you when I get back to my place, but wait to eat, so we can eat together."

"You got it," I say.

He smiles and jogs around to the driver's side of his car.

"Oh, Drew?"

"Yeah?"

"Thank you."

His expression lights up as he nods his head and hops in his car.

Day One

I head back inside and open my meal to see he got me ravioli with meat sauce and garlic bread as well as a house salad. I plate my food and set up my phone in case he wants to FaceTime. I mean, this is a date after all.

While I wait, I cheat and take a peek at what's in the bag he gave the deliveryman. I close my eyes while chuckling to myself after seeing some microwave popcorn, Red Vines, and Peanut M&M's. This must be a dinner and a movie date.

My phone rings, and I see it's Drew calling via Face-Time. I click the green button and smile as his face comes into view.

"Hi," he says, waving to the camera. I can see he's set up in his room with his plate on his lap.

"Thank you so much for dinner." I motion to the spread in front of me.

"I hope I made the right choice. I'm sorry I didn't check first, but I was afraid it would ruin the surprise. My mom said you can't go wrong with ravioli, so I went with her suggestion."

I try to hide the grin spreading across my face. "You asked your mom?"

He chuckles under his breath. "Yes, okay, I did. She thought it was a cute idea too," he says, sitting up straighter, like he's proud of the praise he got. "Do you have a drink?" he asks, searching around the screen.

I hold up my White Claw. "Sure do."

He holds up his beer, and we pretend to cheers. Then, we dive into the yummy food in front of us as we talk about our day and other things.

After dinner, I ask, "So, what did you have in mind with what's in the bag?" I hold it up for him to see.

"You have Netflix, right?" he asks.

"Yeah …" I say, slightly confused.

"We're going to Netflix and chill," he says, shrugging his shoulders.

I let out a sharp laugh. "You do realize what the *chill* part actually means, right?"

His sexy grin makes my heart pound. "Yes, but in our quarantine times, it literally means just chill. If I ask you to though, you have to pretend that I threw some popcorn at you."

"Deal."

"And that I'm holding your hand throughout the movie, okay? Maybe even wrapping my arm around you?"

"Will I get a kiss good night too?" I ask.

He holds up his hands in front of his face. "Whoa, whoa now. Don't move too fast; we just met." He can barely hold his expression from falling into laughter.

"Okay, Drew, let's Netflix and chill."

"You can pick the movie if you want."

I bring my shoulders up to my ears in excitement. "This date just got even better! Romance anyone?"

He smiles and nods. "Romance it is."

Day 6

April 1

My text dings with an incoming message, and I smile brightly when I see Drew's name flash across my screen.

> Drew: They should change the lyrics to this song to, "Wake me up when April ends."

A YouTube link appears on my screen of a couple embracing in Green Day's "Wake Me Up When September Ends" video.

I click the link and watch for over a minute of a couple talking about how much they love each other before the music even starts. When it does, I'm taken to a much different meaning than what I thought the song actually meant. I assumed it was about Hurricane Katrina, but the video shows a young couple in love, and then the guy joins the Army before going off to war.

I text back.

> Me: Wow. Why did I think that song was about Hurricane Katrina? That video was intense.

Drew: Yeah. I just watched it for the first time too. I kind of regret sending it, as it's a little bit of a mood buster.

I look up the song's meaning.

Me: And now, it takes on a whole new meaning even more. Did you know it was actually written for the lead singer's father who died September 1 when he was ten?

Drew: Yep, I keep digging us into a sadder hole. Not my intention, I swear.

Me: It did release right when Katrina happened, so at least I know why I thought that. But look at what I found! You're not the only one who put the song to what's happening now!

I send him a parody song that someone did—"Wake Me Up When Corona Ends."
A few minutes later, he responds.

Drew: Nice! #greatminds

Me: I love that you sent me a song though. This came across my playlist as I was cleaning this morning. With what's going on, it made me pause and take it in.

I send him "Come Around" by Papa Roach. He doesn't respond, and I hope it's because he's watching the link I sent him.

Drew: Now, that's a cool video.

Day One

Me: I love how music can heal people like that.

Drew: Absolutely.

I send a meme I saw about artists that says, *Next time you think being an artist isn't a real career, try to live through this quarantine without music, books, movies, and porn.*

Drew: Porn?

Me: Ha! Yeah, I guess that's considered an art now. ;-)

Drew: So, I was thinking … I'm about to go for a run. I have a key to access the track at the high school. It's about eight feet apart if you stay on the inside and I stay on the outside, so we should be fine. How about you join me?

A sharp laugh escapes my lips.

Me: What is this "run" word you say? I've never heard of such a term. Let me go look it up in the dictionary. Hold, please.

Me: Ha! Just looked up the definition. Yeah, that's something I definitely don't do.

Drew: Ha-ha-ha. Come on. Join me. I'll make it worth your while. ;-)

Me: Winky face? Worth my while? I'm listening.

Drew: The sun is out today, so there's a chance I'll get hot and have to take off my shirt.

Me: Go on.

Drew: I've been told I have quite the abs. What do people say, washboard?

Me: I'm envisioning it … I'm off the couch, but I'll need more to actually get out of my PJs.

Drew: What if I dropped down and did push-ups every time you wanted to stop running?

Me: I'm starting to change …

Drew: I was going to wear basketball shorts, but I do own a pair of gray sweatpants that I hear many girls swoon over.

Me: I'm running out the door!

Drew: <3

Me: Fine. Where should I meet you?

Drew: Pull into the back parking lot. You'll see my car parked near the gate. I'll have it open and ready for you to enter. Then, just walk to the track.

Day One

Me: Could we get in trouble for this? The last thing I need is for my name to appear in a headline about a teacher who was caught trespassing on school grounds with a very hot major league baseball player because she'd passed out due to exhaustion and he had to call an ambulance. Because that ambulance thing could totally happen. Don't be surprised. You've been warned!

Drew: I was given a key by Coach Thompson. I promise we won't get in trouble.

Me: Give me ten.

Drew: That really means, like, fifteen to twenty, right?

Me: Good boy. This thing we have going on is really on the right track.

Drew: ;-)

I throw my phone on my couch and head to my room to start getting ready for what I'm sure will be an absolute butt-kicking.

When I arrive at the high school, I see the gate slightly open with his car parked right next to it. I park and make my way through the entrance and to the bleachers, heading to the track.

He doesn't notice I'm here yet, so I take this opportunity to really check him out for the first time. He did in fact wear his gray sweatpants along with a sleeveless shirt. The way his pants hug him in all the right places makes my chest tighten.

He's wearing the same ball cap he wore in the first picture he sent me. I don't know why, but that makes me smile. I've always envisioned a down-home country boy with his favorite cap as one of my dream guys, and yet here's this professional baseball player standing in front of me. He's not country. He's not down-home. But yet that cap … it's perfect.

I open the gate more, and it catches his attention.

He jogs toward me and then stops and grins from ear to ear. "Hi." He waves, and it's the cutest, most awkward thing ever.

"You know, I'm sure it's okay if we stand next to each other. I'm not that worried about it," I say as I take a step closer.

We're still ten feet apart at least.

His expression falls. "I really wish that were the case, but with my mom"—he takes a deep breath—"I just can't risk anything."

My heart swoons at his concern over his mother. I smile big. "Then, at least six feet apart we shall stay."

He nods and pulls up his right leg behind him, stretching his quads. When I don't follow his lead, he eyes me. "It's good to stretch and warm up your legs before we jump in."

I sigh and do as he does. "You're lucky you even got me out here. Don't push your luck, golden boy."

His smirk is priceless at my choice of nickname for him that I read online.

He runs me through some stretches and warms us up before he says, "Okay, you ready?"

I close my eyes and shake my head. "Why am I doing this?"

"Because you like me?"

My lids fly open, and I'm graced with the most handsome face I've ever seen grinning back at me.

"Maybe." I point my finger at him. "We'll see how I feel after this attack on my lungs."

He tilts his head to the side, showing which way he wants to run, and I begrudgingly move my feet.

Thankfully, he starts off slow, and I find a rhythm.

"So, what kind of music do you normally listen to?" he asks like we're sitting on the couch in my living room and not running around a track.

I give him the evil eye. "I. Can't. Really. Talk. Right. Now," I say a word at a time through each breath.

He laughs, and to my surprise, he slows down. "Then, let's not run so fast. In order to keep a good pace that you can sustain for a long time, you should be able to hold a conversation during your run."

We proceed, and I thankfully find it more doable, so I finally answer him, "I like everything."

He turns to me in question.

"Music, I mean. I loved that concert each artist did from their homes the other day on TV. When it went from Billie Joe to Tim McGraw, I was in heaven."

"Were you screaming like a little girl when the Backstreet Boys came on?" he teases.

I laugh—well, as much as I can while barely being able to breathe. "Um, no. Thankfully, my sister was never into them, and they were before my time, so I never had the boy-band crushes."

"Who are your crushes then?"

"What?" I dramatically pull back my head while facing him. "Besides the Major League Baseball player I just met? Hmm." I pretend I'm thinking.

His laugh tickles my ears, and I almost trip over myself.

He jogs a little faster and then turns around, so he's running backward, and we're facing each other. "Did you really not know who I was?"

"And there it is. I knew you had to have a big head tucked under that sexy ball cap."

He chuckles, and I have to stop, needing the rest. He does, too, and instantly drops to the ground, doing push-ups.

I giggle under my breath. "You were serious about that?"

He continues his ups and downs without looking up. "Dead serious. It will be a good workout for me in the end, kind of a cross-training thing. I do have to be fit for my job, you know," he says through a laugh.

I cross my arms in front of my body and take in the way his muscles bulge as he moves with ease. "Then, you'll do those until I'm ready to run again?"

"Yep," he says, but I can hear in his voice that he's starting to strain.

"Hmm," I tease. "So … what do you think about the weather? Do you think it will stay nice like this or start to rain again?"

He pops up to his feet so fast that I'm caught off guard. "Nice try. Let's go."

He runs again, and I follow, pretending to hate it but, deep down, this is the best time I've ever had exercising. Who knows? This might become my favorite pastime.

Okay, not really. I haven't lost my marbles that much yet.

"Hey, I think I was supposed to get the view of you shirtless too," I call after him.

He takes his shirt off and throws it my way.

Okay, yeah, I was wrong. This is *definitely* becoming my favorite pastime.

Day 7

April 2

After I hop out of the shower, I dry myself off and hear my phone ring. The sound of "Centerfield" by John Fogerty plays with the familiar clapping and then a guitar riff that I dance to for a beat before I answer by singing, " *'Put me in, Coach. I'm ready to play today.'* "

Drew laughs out loud. "You did not."

"Oh, I sure did. So, if it takes me a while to answer your call, just know that I'm over here, dancing to your ring-tone."

"You crack me up," he says.

"Thank you, thank you. I'll be here all day because, well, you know, nowhere else to go and all."

"That's why I'm calling. I had an idea."

"I'm all ears!"

"Let's go for a drive to the lake," he says, his tone full of hopefulness.

"Um ... I thought you wanted to keep your distance because of your mom?"

"Yes, that's why you'll stay in your car, and I'll be in mine while we FaceTime the entire way."

"You're too cute."

"Do you have enough gas?"

"Even better. I drive a Nissan LEAF, so no need for gas here."

"Great. Then, I'll be there shortly."

He calls when he pulls up twenty minutes later. "Are you ready?"

I step out into my garage where the large door is already up, smiling when he comes into view, standing by his car.

"Let's do this," I say into the phone.

Seeing his smile is exactly what I imagine every time we speak on the phone.

He nods. "Okay, follow me."

I hang up and get in my car, backing out of my driveway and positioning myself behind him. We get on the road, and before we get to the end of my block, my phone rings with a FaceTime call.

I answer with a smile, "Wow, what a surprise! Long time no see."

He chuckles, slightly shaking his head at my antics. "Is there a place to rest your phone, so we can still see each other but you're not distracted while driving?"

I place it in my cupholder, which makes the phone face low and up for him to see me. "Well, not the most flattering view," I tease.

"Any view is flattering when it comes to you," he says.

It's a totally adorable statement, but I can't let him get away with it completely. It's in my nature to play with him a little. "Aw, aren't you flattering with your pick-up lines."

"I have plenty, so just you wait." He grins while keeping his eyes on the road.

Day One

We get on the freeway that surprisingly still has a decent amount of people on it.

Aren't we supposed to be on lockdown? Ha! Asks the girl who's literally driving right next to these people. But we're doing it safely, in different cars, and I don't even feel bad about it since I drive an electric.

I nod my head, agreeing with myself.

"What should we listen to?" Drew asks.

Knowing that he's right in front of me yet also right next to me on the phone makes me laugh. *Technology these days ...*

"Why don't we turn on the rock station?" I suggest. "The stations that play the popular music nowadays cycle through, like, ten songs over and over again, and it's super annoying."

"Yes! Why is that?"

"Who knows? But I can barely stand some of it, so after the second time, I want to throw my radio out the window."

"Rock it is!"

We both click the radio on and listen to see what's playing. "Cut the Cord" by Shinedown begins, and I reach over to turn it up. I bob my head to the beat and start to sing under my breath to the words as we make our way down the freeway.

I laugh out loud when I hear Drew shout, " *'Cut the cord!'* "

So, I join in, " *'Freedom, la-la-la-la. Freedom.'* "

"Nice." He stares into the screen for a brief second.

As the song ends, he turns down his radio and speaks up, "Okay, game time. What's one song that you can sing from start to finish?"

My eyes widen as all of the best choices race through my head. *Should it be a rock song? Or how about a country one? No, I'm going old-school rap on this one. He wants a game? Oh, he's going to get a game.*

"What do you know about Andre Nickatina?"

"Oh no, you didn't!" He covers his mouth in a *holy shit* kind of way.

"I'm a Bay Area girl, remember? 'Smoke Dope and Rap' all the way. Bring it, baby."

"Well, you're in luck. I just so happen to have that on my playlist, which is loaded into my stereo system."

I sigh dreamily. "We really are a match made in heaven."

He winks at the phone, and I'm so glad I caught the action.

The familiar sound of a phone ringing starts, and I sit up straight when I shout, " *'Hey, Pook, get the phone!'* " which is how the song starts off. " *'Who dis, man?'* " I say in my manliest tone. " *'Ready, go, man!'* " I shout out as the beat drops.

I flow with the lyrics, bouncing around with each phrase, like I'm a rapper onstage at a big show.

I don't miss a beat while I bust it out, but when I get to my favorite part of the song, I look right into the phone and sing, " *'Oh, it's Jeannine. She lick my dick clean.'* "

Drew cracks up, and his laughter screws up my flow as I break out in giggles.

"You messed me up!"

"I know, but come on, how could I not?" he says through his chuckles.

We play his game a few more times, but none are as funny as mine. When we pull up to the lake, I realize how long we were on the road but how fast the time went by.

We park and walk, separated, to the lake.

"Isn't this technically against our shelter-in-place order?" I ask, eyeing him suspiciously.

"I read that some head guy who works for the county brought his family out to the beach a few days ago. They were dumb enough to post pics to social media. We won't do that." He grins.

"That didn't really answer my question."

"Yeah, but if we don't get caught ..." He raises his eyebrows. "Besides, there's no one here, so we're fine."

"There's no one here because they're all following the rules and staying home," I joke.

"But not everyone is trying to win the heart of a new girl, so desperate times call for desperate measures."

I grin in his direction. "Okay then, you're off the hook."

When we get close to the water, he places the bag that he took out of his car on the ground and takes out two towels. He lays one down and then steps a few feet—okay, a lot of feet—away and lays another one down. I try not to laugh at how silly this is, but I guess it's our new normal, and knowing his mom has a compromised immune system, it's well worth it.

I watch as he sets a bag on what I'm thinking is my towel and then takes his bag over to his spot.

"What's in the bag?" I ask.

"I brought us lunch."

He sits on his towel, so I make my way to mine.

"What's on the menu, sir?" I ask, acting dignified with an accent.

"PB and J." His expression makes me giggle as he holds up the sandwich in a ziplock baggie. "And"—he sticks his finger in the air before he takes out one item at a time—"a fruit cup, chips, and"—he pauses for dramatic effect before he pulls the last item out—"a White Claw, just for you."

"My dream lunch!" I celebrate overdramatically, but I'm being honest. This is just my type of food, especially with the White Claw to top it off.

We sit on our own towels while we talk and eat our lunch. Every second that passes by, I feel more comfortable with him. He tells me about his time in the minor leagues—holy hell, I had no idea how crazy that could be—and then I tell him about why I went into teaching.

Afterward, we go to the water, and he teaches me how to skip rocks. We take off our shoes and stick our feet in the lake. With the sun on our backs, the cool water actually feels good.

We spend all day like that, together yet apart.

When I realize it's Thursday, I have to pause and reflect. Talk about finding the bright side to a really shitty situation. On any other day, I would be walking out of my classroom, heading home and trying to figure out what to do for dinner, all while being alone.

Now, here I am with a guy I'm really starting to fall for, lying next to a lake and feeling happier than ever. Funny how the world works.

Would Drew have even opened up his Tinder app if it weren't for this quarantine? Probably not. He'd be playing baseball, traveling to who knows where.

It's hard to be thankful for such a horrible situation, but I'd be lying to myself if I didn't at least think that. I guess everything happens for a reason, and for me, this was the universe's way of introducing me to Drew.

I tilt my head and say a silent thank-you to whoever is listening before turning my attention back to the gorgeous man sitting eight feet away.

Day 8

April 3

My new favorite song blares through my phone, and I clap myself on the back for changing Drew's ringtone.

"Well, good morning," I sing into the phone.

"Good morning, sunshine. What are you up to?" he asks, sounding so upbeat that I can't help but smile bigger.

"You'll never guess what I just did."

"What?" he says like a kid who's dying to know a really big secret.

"I went for a run. All by myself!" I say so proudly that I could burst.

He laughs under his breath. "You did not," he says in disbelief.

"I totally did."

"I have to admit, I'm proud of you. Good job."

"I had to! I was watching that show *WAGS* last night, and it got me thinking. If this really goes somewhere between us and I'm going to date a Major League Baseball player, I have to step up my game to be able to fight off any girls who think they can take my spot."

There it is. That deep belly laugh I love on him so much.

"I don't think you have to worry about that."

"Have you *seen* that show?" I ask, dramatically. "Bitches be crazy when it comes to their men. Are you forgetting I'm just a little ole elementary teacher over here?"

"Sharee, you're more than any one of those girls or the other girls I've ever met."

I normally come back with something snarky or playful, but in this moment, I'm speechless. Hearing him say that melts my heart.

"I think I like you, Drew Miller," I say.

"Right back at you, kid."

"Okay, so now that that's out of the way"—I giggle—"what are you doing today?"

"I'm lying in my bed now, thinking of you, of course."

My chest instantly tightens, and my core tingles. "Okay, deep breath to get through that thought. Inhale"—I exaggerate the noise—"and exhale." I blow out into the phone. "Okay, I'm good. Continue."

His breathy laugh tickles my ear.

I swear I'm a goner for this guy.

"I have to get up pretty quickly though to get ready for a Skype interview with ESPN."

"*Oh, you know, I'm just going to be on national television when ninety percent of the world is home and most of the dudes are watching ESPN, dying for sports entertainment. No biggie,*" I say in my manliest tone.

"And thank you for adding that level of nervousness to my morning," he states matter of factly.

"I'm sorry. Are you really nervous?" I curl up on my couch, wanting to comfort him.

A sharp laugh escapes his lips. "Of course I am. Wouldn't you be?"

"I just figured it was something you'd be used to by now."

"No," he says slowly. "I just want to play baseball. All the other stuff is hard on me."

"But you did that video for the kids."

Yes, I've watched that video a few times. He seemed so relaxed and comfortable in front of the camera.

"Yeah, but that was for kids. I can talk to kids all day about baseball. They're still excited about the game. As you get older, it changes. Money gets involved, and things get skewed."

"The money bothers you, doesn't it?"

He sighs. "I can't say I'm not happy to finally be making a good paycheck, but it adds another layer. More pressure, I guess. I've been playing this entire time to prove to myself that I could make a pro team. Now, I feel like I have to prove myself to earn my paycheck. And believe me, people remind you of that all the time."

I sit silently, not sure what to say, when he says, "Wow, I sound like a whiny little bitch. I'm sorry."

"No. Don't ever be sorry for sharing with me. I love that you even consider things like this. You can be open with me about everything."

"And that's what I like about you. I feel comfortable enough to do so."

"Aw, he likes me; he really likes me," I say, making a joke, like I always do. Then, something comes to my mind. "So, you don't mind talking to kids then?"

"Why?" he asks, sounding suspicious.

He knows me so well already!

"I have a Zoom meeting with my class today. I know a few of them would die if you joined in. What do you say?"

"I'd love to!" he says, not hiding his excitement.

"Seriously?"

"Yes, seriously. I remember all the players I looked up to when I was in sixth grade. I would have died if I'd gotten a chance to talk to them. This," he says as a statement all on its own, "is the part of the job I love."

This guy just keeps getting better and better.

"Well, you're about to make me the best teacher around. What's your email address? I'll send you the Zoom link."

"It's Drew24baseball at gmail dot com."

"Twenty-four? Is that your number?"

"Sure is. Thankfully, I'm able to keep it too."

"I bet it took on a whole new meaning after Kobe passed," I say, somber.

"You have no idea. I chose twenty-four because of Ken Griffey Jr. and Rickey Henderson. After hearing Kobe chose it because he said it took twenty-four/seven to make it, I loved it even more. He's right. It's a never-ending grind, and you have to love it enough to push harder."

"You really love it, don't you?"

"Every. Damn. Second," he says with a pleased sigh.

I smile at his statement.

"Okay, I lied. Except the interview parts," he corrects.

I laugh. "Go get ready. I'll be watching."

"And the nerves keep getting stronger. You're not very good at this, you know."

"Go get 'em, big boy!" I holler. "I'll send you the link too. Zoom is at eleven. I'll text you when it's okay to get on, so I can get through the important stuff, and then you'll be the surprise at the end."

"I like being a surprise."

"You've been my surprise through all of this," I say with a grin.

"And you're mine. See you soon. Bye," he says.

And what is it about the way that guys say *bye* that turns me on so much? It's like this level of anticipation that keeps you waiting for more until you talk to them next. And damn, he says the best *bye* for sure.

Day One

After I hang up, I call my sister, Shelly. I told her I met a guy, but I failed to fill her in on who this guy even is.

"Hey," she says as she answers the phone. "What's going on?"

"Is Matthew around?" I ask.

"Ha! Where's he supposed to be besides home?" she taunts.

I shake my head at my sister's words. "I meant, is he near you?"

"He's in his room. Do you want me to get him?"

"Yeah, go get him and put me on speakerphone."

I hear her walking through the house as she heads toward his room.

"Okay, he's with me. What's up?" she asks.

"Shelly, do you remember the guy I told you I met on Tinder the other day?" I ask.

"Um, not sure if Matthew should be hearing this, so please proceed with caution," Shelly says in her most motherly tone.

"Oh, come on. I'm not that bad," I plead.

"Don't make me remind you about that last guy you dated," she says through a laugh.

I shake my entire body to rid the memory of the mechanic who liked to play with tools inside and *outside* of the shop in ways that were a little questionable to everyone involved.

"Fine," I say, giving in. "But I promise this is different. Matthew, do you recognize the name Andrew Miller?"

"Shut up, Auntie Sharee," Matthew says, making me smile.

"Who's Andrew?" Shelly asks.

"Mom, he just signed with the Giants," Matthew says. "He used to play with the Titans too. Coach talked about trying to get him to come out to one of our practices since he's local now."

"I bet we can get him to do that," I say playfully.

"Wait, so you're dating a baseball player? Who you met on Tinder?" Shelly asks in disbelief.

"I know, right? I'm shocked too. I had no idea he was a player. He's going live on ESPN in a little while. Go turn it on."

"I will," Matthew yells out.

"We'll both watch," Shelly says and then turns the speakerphone off and brings the phone to her ear. "So, you're really talking with this guy?"

"I'm more than talking. We're dating. Shelly, he's so amazing. It's been the best few days ever."

I tell her about our time together and how great it's been.

"I'm so happy for you," she says.

"Thanks, sis. Okay, I have to shower. I have a Zoom meeting with my students, and he's going to surprise them."

"Wow, your popularity with some kids is going to shoot through the roof."

"I know. I'm so excited to see their faces! Love ya!" I say before she replies the same, and then we hang up.

After I shower, I stay glued to ESPN, waiting for his interview to come on, checking a hundred times to make sure it's recording. When they tease that he's coming up, I jump with excitement and run to take my spot on the couch.

They split the screen with the host, and there, on national TV, is the guy I'm falling hard for. He looks so handsome with his hair done and a casual T-shirt on. Even the bad angle of the computer camera doesn't hurt how handsome he is.

When the host introduces him, his grin and silly wave make me giggle like a twelve-year-old girl watching her favorite crush on television.

Day One

Oh my God, my tween girlie dreams have come true. I'm actually dating the cute guy on TV!

The host asks questions about the season and how Drew feels about finally getting his big break, only to be sent home on quarantine. I can see that tiny bit of nervousness he talked about. It's so stinking adorable that I can barely contain myself.

I'm distracted when an alert for a text goes off.

Shelly: Oh, he's cute!

Me: I know! Leave me alone. I'm watching.

I curl my legs up on my couch, so I'm sitting cross-legged, and I lean forward. My cheeks are starting to hurt because I have such a big smile on my face.

"So, tell me, Andrew," the host says. "What are you doing during this time?"

The handsomest smile grows across his face, and I can tell he's trying not to laugh. My chest pounds as I wait for his answer.

"Well, Sam, I actually met a girl and, um ..."

The host laughs. "You met someone during the quarantine?"

He joins in with his own laugh. "Yep, sure did." He shrugs. "It's been a fun time, getting to know her—while keeping our distance, of course."

The host nods while dropping his head slightly to hide his chuckle. "Instead of dating in the twenty-first century, it's turned into dating during a quarantine."

Drew laughs. "Yeah, pretty much."

"We wish you luck with both the new season and this new girl. Thanks for taking the time to chat with us."

"No problem. Thanks for having me."

He disappears from the screen, and I scream out loud.

My phone rings automatically, showing my sister's name.

"He just talked about you on TV!" she says in celebration.

"I know! I'm freaking out."

We chat about all the ways I'm super excited until I have to hang up to get ready for my Zoom meeting.

Before I do, I send a text to Drew.

> Me: So, this girl you're seeing …

> Drew: Yeah?

> Me: She'd better be hot. Don't settle for anything less. You're a pro now!

> Drew: Oh, don't you worry. She's the sexiest woman I've ever met.

Be still my heart.

> Me: <3

> Me: I'm about to log on to Zoom. I'll text you when I'm ready.

> Drew: I'll be here!

In front of my students, it's hard to contain the anticipation racing through me as I go over the plans for the day and give mini math lessons. Then, I answer any questions the students might have.

I send Drew a text to log on, and within seconds, a new screen pops up.

"Okay, everyone, I have a little surprise for you. Nick, this one's especially for you."

Day One

Nick, thankfully, pays closer attention, as it's obvious he's been playing video games while we've been chatting. Nice to know he's at least listening.

"Yeah?" he asks.

I click Drew's screen and make him the feature view. "Class, we have a special visitor today. I'd like you all to meet Andrew Miller."

"Wait, what?" Nick yells, and he's suddenly facing the screen, giving us his full attention.

"Hey, everyone!" Drew says, waving to the class.

"Who's Andrew Miller?" Mandy, one of the students, asks.

"He just signed with the Giants, Mandy," Nick answers for us.

"Yes. Yes, I did. How many baseball or softball players do we have in here?"

A few kids raise their hands.

"Are you bummed like me that your season has been put on hold?"

"Yes!" Nick shouts. "I watched your video, and my dad helped me set up an area in our backyard, so I can continue to work. Thanks for doing that."

"Nice. Glad to know it helped," Drew replies.

I sit back and watch as the students each take turns in asking questions. Drew comes off cool and laid-back, and I can see the difference he talked about between chatting with the media and with kids. He's a natural with kids, and even ones who I know don't follow sports are captivated as they listen to him talk.

Hell, I am too.

Only for different reasons than them. While they're staring at someone they admire, I'm staring at someone who might just be the addition I've been wanting in my life.

Day 9

April 4

I stare outside at the rainy day. Now, not only am I stuck at my house, but I'm also stuck inside.

I thought about going for another run despite the rain, but I was afraid I'd slip and break an ankle. There's no way I'm going to the doctor for anything, so, yeah, my pledge to start running every day lasted one whole day.

I'd like to say I'll start back up when the rain stops, but the forecast shows it's going to rain until Tuesday. By then, I'll have long forgotten about the fact that, yes, I *can* physically run—plus, you know, getting back on the bandwagon is much harder the second time.

I sigh. I'll have to fight off the wannabe WAGs with my charm and brains rather than my sexy body because, let's face it, I'm going to gain weight while we're in this predicament. I might as well accept that fact and move on to enjoy the snacks I bought.

When my phone rings with my favorite tune, I do a happy dance and answer, admitting my failure right off the bat, "My running streak is off, so don't judge."

Day One

Drew chuckles under his breath. "No judgment here. I'll just leave you with the song by Papa Roach. *'You gotta want it. You gotta want it,'* " he sings out.

"Ugh, you suck, you know that?" I taunt.

"But seriously, don't do it for me. I already think you're sexy as hell. I loved working out with you the other day, but only do it if you want to and for no one else."

"It was nice, watching you do all those push-ups ..." I smile big.

"And see, I could only do them because you had to stop so many times. If you get better at running, then I won't get the upper-body workout I need."

"Now, I feel so much better," I say, exaggerating. "Just know, when I'm lying on my ass, eating ice cream, I'm doing it for you."

He laughs. "Great teamwork. But hey, you know what I learned today?" he says like he's proud to share his findings.

"What?" I ask in the same tone.

"That you can't spell virus without *U* and *I*."

Now, it's my turn to let out a belly-laugh at one of his jokes. "You're too cute. Did you make that one up all on your own?"

He sighs. "I can't take any credit for that one. I saw it online. But technically, I am your Prince Charmin because I brought you toilet paper on our first date."

"Indeed, you did! Here I've always thought it was Prince Charming," I say, enunciating the last part.

"What will all those Disney princesses do, knowing they didn't need some guy to climb up their hair or kiss them to wake them out of a spell? Those damn girls just needed toilet paper."

I slap my hand on the couch when I sit up as it comes to me. "Oh my God, they totally did! After the first kiss, you know they went straight to doing the horizontal tango, and they needed the toilet paper to clean up the mess! Drew, you just solved all the problems of the world right there."

He's laughing so hard that I can hear he's having a hard time breathing. "Did you really say *horizontal tango*?"

"It is a Disney flick after all. I can't just come out and say they went in there and he fucked her so hard that she couldn't close her legs for a week," I deadpan. "These are kid shows, for goodness' sake."

"You are too much," he says through his laughter. "So, you're saying that toilet paper saved the day? Not the kiss from a prince?"

"I'm saying," I drawl out, "the kiss leads to the fucking, which leads to the mess. So, yeah, toilet paper saved the day. Guys have no clue how much of a mess sex actually is. Us girls have to stand up and do this squishy walk-run thing to the bathroom before everything escapes and slides down our legs. Then, don't even ask me about the stuff that falls to our asses. I feel like I'm wiping an entire gallon of self-lube afterward. It's really not pretty."

"Hey, that would be all from you, so you shouldn't complain. Self-lube from the female says the guy was doing something right. Unless you're a squirter." He pauses. "Oh my God, do you squirt when you come?"

"Hello!" I announce. "If I squirted, all that liquid would go forward, not down my crack."

"So, you're saying you have no problem with what you call *self-lube*, huh?" he asks, changing his tone to one that's sultrier.

"Wow, way to change the subject quickly but slyly," I tease.

"Hey, you're talking about sex to a guy who's on lockdown in his parents' home after he's been on the road, living on his own since he was eighteen. My mind will absolutely wander in that direction, especially because I'm calling you from my car in front of your house."

I sit up and run to the window. "You're here?"

"Yeah. I wasn't sure if you had a mask, like the government is recommending we wear if we leave the house."

"Did you bring me one?" I ask, surprised by how sweet that thought is.

"My mom loves to sew, and when we saw the press conference last night, saying people should wear them, she got to work on making them for all of our loved ones."

"And you had her make me one?" I'm not going to lie; my voice might have cracked slightly at my question.

I can only imagine the grin I hope is covering his face right now. I'm staring at him through the window, but with how my place is situated on the street, I can only see parts of him through the passenger window.

"You should have seen her face when I asked her to. Let's just say, my parents don't hear me talk about girls often ... pretty much never."

"So, you're not the guy who brings your girlfriends home to meet the 'rents?"

" 'Rents?"

"Come on. We aren't that old. Parents. 'Rents. It's cool-dude lingo. Keep up," I state matter-of-factly.

"Then, no, the *'rents* don't know much about my dating life."

"Ugh! I knew you were too good to be true. You're a *love 'em and leave 'em* kind of guy, aren't you?"

He chuckles. "No, I'm a *girls are too much of a distraction, and I have goals I need to reach* kind of guy."

"And now that you've reached those goals ..." I leave the question open.

"Time to find out what I've been missing."

My hand covers my chest as I feel my heart beat faster and faster.

"So, yeah, you've made my mom's day. I'm an only child, and now that I'm home and signed to a team, she says she wants grandkids."

"Is there a guy version of the scene from *My Cousin Vinny*?" I ask, trying to hold back my giggle.

"No," he says, laughing.

"Then, that's all you want from me? My womb, so you can get your mom off your back?" I fake being angry.

"And all you want is my toilet paper!" he fights back, and I fall over, laughing.

"Okay, you win. That was a good one."

He pauses, and as I take some deep breaths, I have to purposely elongate my face, so my cheeks don't hurt.

"I'm sorry, and I hate to have to run, but I have some masks to deliver. I'm going to leave yours on your front porch, okay?"

"Sounds good. Please tell your mom I said thank you."

"I will. Bye, Sharee."

"Bye, Drew."

I watch as he exits his car and races toward my house, so he doesn't get caught in the rain. I run to my door, dying to open it, throw my arms around him, and see just how wet he can really make me, but I don't. Instead, I spy on him through the peephole, shamelessly checking out every inch of him.

"I know you're behind that door, watching me," he says.

"No, I'm not," I state.

He leans up to the peephole and kisses it. It's a quick movement, but I nearly become weak in the knees in glee. It's our first kiss and one I'll never forget!

Day 10

April 5

My phone dings with an incoming text message. I was so fond of my ringtone that I looked for what I could use for Drew when it came to text messages as well. Imagine my excitement when I found the sound of a ball being hit off a bat! Now, every time my messages go off, all I can imagine is the sight of his arms swinging a large wooden bat and then him running down the field.

I can imagine it because I've seen it. It's amazing what you can find on the internet when you have all the time in the world to devote to searching—not snooping on—someone.

Okay, who am I kidding? I was totally snooping, but who wouldn't?

I even found a YouTube video from years ago when he was being scouted. Seeing the baby-faced Drew was so adorable. They did little interviews with him and showed just about every at-bat or dig that he made at first base.

And look at me, using the word *dig* when it comes to catching a ball. Yeah, I looked that up too. I'm going to be the most amazing, supportive WAG there.

I can envision it now. I'll have on his jersey—which I've looked for and they don't have available yet. Don't get me started on that. And I'm hoping he can get me close, so I can be there, cheering him on for every game I can go to. And, yes, I plan on making a sign that says, *That's my man!*

I wonder if he'll think that's too much.

Nah, he'll expect nothing less from me, I'm sure. Then, all the other guys will ask why their WAGs aren't as supportive as I am, and I'll start this huge issue between the players and their wives.

Okay, maybe that's a little too far, I'll admit. I'll just start with his jersey and make my way up to the sign.

I grab my phone and swipe it on to read his text.

Drew: How about we make dinner together tonight?

Me: Of course. When and where?

Me: Oh, wait, we're on lockdown. I'm curious, how is this going to work?

Drew: We're going to cook together via FaceTime. I'm going to bring you the groceries and drop them off on your porch.

Me: Love it! I'll be here.

Drew: Okay, I'll be there shortly.

I race around and actually get ready like I would if it were a real date. I blow-dry my light brown hair and do my makeup. I know he's seen me in my current state, but he hasn't seen me at my best. I want to dress up to show my appreciation toward him for our so-called date.

Day One

An hour later, I hear a knock on my door. I race to it and open it up. Drew is already back to his car, but he waits for me.

I stand there in my favorite spring dress even though the rain is misting around us. A cold breeze washes over me, but it's nothing compared to the tingles running over my body from seeing him.

His eyes light up. "You look amazing," he says breathlessly.

I grin and blink my eyes. "Thank you. You're not so bad-looking yourself."

He has on my favorite cap and a fitted, long-sleeved henley that hugs him in the best way—not too tight or too loose, just perfect.

"Everything you need is in there." He points to the bag on my porch. "I'll call you when I get home."

I wave, and he returns the gesture before driving off.

I grab the bag and take it inside, wondering what's in store for tonight.

I can't help but laugh at the items as I remove each one. He should have known I have salt and pepper, but he took no chances. Absolutely everything I need to make dinner is in this bag, including a bottle of wine.

When my phone rings, I click the green button to answer on FaceTime.

"Hey there, beautiful," he says, and I have to stop myself from swooning since he can see me.

I'm standing at my kitchen counter, so I lean down and put my chin on my hand, tilting my head to the side. "What are we cookin', good-lookin'?"

"I didn't want you to have to do a ton of dishes, so I got a one-pot recipe from my mom."

"That's so cute," I say.

"Oh, yeah? You like that?"

I nod with a grin on my face.

"Well, how about the fact that she's right here, guiding me, so I don't screw things up?"

I stand up straight, surprised and a little scared, to say the least. Meeting the parents is a big deal. Thank God I look my best for this date!

"Your mom's there?" I ask, trying to fake nonchalance.

He flips the camera, so I can see who's sitting at the end of the counter. "Say hi, Mom."

"Hi, Sharee." She waves. "We're super excited to meet you. I'm Pamela."

I wave into the camera. "Hello! It's so nice to meet you too. You've done well, raising the young gentleman you have there."

She smiles from ear to ear. "We're very proud of our boy."

Drew flips the camera back to him. "And that's enough of that." He chuckles nervously. "I'm going to prop the camera up right here, so we can work together. Can you see me okay?"

"Sure can." I do the same and then reach for the bottle. "So, first step is to open the bottle of wine, right?" I ask playfully.

He points into the camera. "Yes! Okay." He moves around the kitchen, searching for an opener.

I can tell he's out of his element, and it's freaking adorable. His mom finally comes to his rescue and hands him the opener. He thanks her and proceeds to open the bottle and pour some into a glass.

"Cheers," he says as he holds it up to me.

"Cheers," I reply, trying to hide how happy this moment is making me.

"Okay, do you have all of your ingredients ready?" he asks, rubbing his hands together like he's about to dive deep into a project.

I nod. "The contents of your bag cracked me up. I'm pretty sure I already had salt and pepper."

I hear his mom laugh. "You bought her salt and pepper too?"

He shrugs. "Hey, I didn't know. I've been living probably the worst bachelor life you can think of for the last eight years. I didn't want to assume anything."

His expression is priceless.

"Now, first things first. We have to cut the chicken into tiny pieces and cook it. Oh, wait." He holds up a finger.

He reaches for something. When I see him slip an apron over his head and tie it around his waist, I almost fall over from laughing. The black apron has a pig on it and says, *Every butt deserves a good rub.*

"Where did you find that?" I ask.

He shows it off by pulling his shoulders back. "Online. I had it overnighted."

"On a Sunday?" I question.

"Yes, thank God for Amazon. You should have seen some of the ones I found." He nudges his thumb to where his mom is sitting. "I couldn't get those though. You know, with my mom here and all."

"Oh, you have to give me at least one. You can't leave me hanging like that."

"Mom, cover your ears," he shouts and then leans in. "One favorite was, *Once you put my meat in your mouth, you're gonna want to swallow.*"

I nearly spit out my wine, covering my mouth so I don't choke.

"And another one said, *May I suggest the sausage?* And it had a big finger pointing down." His head tilts down with a shit-eating grin on his face, and his eyebrows are raised when he looks back to the camera.

"Andrew." I can hear his mom laugh while pretending to be offended.

"Hey, I didn't buy those! I'm the good guy who chose this one"—he comes close to the camera—"when I really wanted the other ones." He winks.

We continue to cook together, his mom guiding him and then him guiding me. It's obvious where Drew gets his laid-back personality. Getting to listen to the way his mom and him interact is the best part of my night. I can tell they have a good relationship, and it makes me like him that much more.

After our chicken is cooked, we remove it, putting it on a plate, and begin to cook some onions and garlic. Once that's nice and fragrant, we put some pasta in the same pan along with chicken broth and cover the dish, letting the pasta cook.

Drew grabs his glass and stands back to relax and take a sip.

"Okay, Pamela, it's our chance," I say a little louder to make sure she can hear me.

She comes into view.

"Tell me about Drew as a little boy. Oh, and pictures. Yes, I need to see them!"

She giggles as she runs her fingers through his hair, fixing a strand that's gone wild. "Our Andrew was always a ham. Any chance he could get in front of a camera, he did." Her face beams with pride. "I'll make sure to have every-thing ready for when you're finally able to come over for dinner in person."

"Oh no, you won't," Drew states firmly. "We don't need to have Andrew flashbacks."

"Yes, we do!" Pamela and I say at the same time.

He laughs into his wine as he shakes his head and takes a drink. "I'm in trouble with the two of you, aren't I?"

"Yep!" we both say.

"Is this Sharee?" I hear a man's voice say. He walks into the frame and waves.

"Sharee, this is my dad, Tom."

"Hi, Tom."

"It's nice to meet you, Sharee. Sorry I'm late to the party. I was watching the golf match."

"From 2017." Drew laughs.

He shrugs. "It's still golf. I didn't remember exactly who'd won."

Pamela grabs Tom by the arm. "Come on. Let's leave them alone."

"Don't we get food too?" Tom asks.

"Yes, but it's not quite ready yet. We'll take ours in the living room, so they can have the kitchen."

"Boy, you're home for two weeks and already taking over my house again," Tom jokes and then turns to me. "It's nice to meet you, Sharee. Can't wait to meet you in person."

"You too, Tom."

They exit, and Drew heads to the fridge to get the cheese and cream. We prepare the remaining ingredients, and once the pasta is done, we combine it all together and add the fresh spinach at the end.

The meal looks delicious and smells even better! We dish up and both grab our glasses of wine, heading to our tables.

As we eat, all I can think of is how amazing this date has been, and he's not even physically here. It doesn't matter though. I've never felt so comfortable or so engaged when first dating someone. Each day just gets better and better, and I almost never want this quarantine to end.

Almost.

Day 11

April 6

"I had an idea," Drew says as I answer the phone. His excitement is contagious.

"Okay ..." I say, honestly dying to know what he's thinking.

"Is your nephew around today? If I could promise a way to not get close to him, would your sister allow you to bring him out to the junior high? There's a batting cage in the back where we can work."

I stop and think for a second. "Wait, are you asking to hang out with my nephew instead of me?"

He chuckles under his breath. "You would bring him, obviously."

"Then, you're using me to get to him?" I ask exaggeratedly.

"No, I'm using him to get to hang out with you."

"Okay, that's more like it. Let me ask. I'm sure my sister is dying to get him out of the house."

"Great! Let's plan on one. I can meet you guys there. And hey, I know it's kind of weird, but if you want to invite that kid from your class, too, he's welcome."

"Nick? I can always try. His parents think baseball is life, so I'm sure they'd be excited."

"Because baseball *is* life. Don't get that twisted."

"Whatever you say, big man. See you soon."

I hang up and call my sister. "Hey, would Matthew want to go play some baseball with Drew at the junior high?" I ask like I'm asking him to go for a walk, not practice with a Major League Baseball player.

The sharp laugh that escapes her lips makes me giggle. "Are you kidding me?"

"He said he'll promise they'll be safe."

"I think you just made his year. I'm sure he'll be down."

I smile big because Drew's made my year too.

"He said to meet him at one. I'll see you there."

I send an email to Nick's parents with the invitation and details and am surprised when I hear back right away, saying how excited they are for the opportunity.

When we arrive at the junior high, Drew is there with three buckets of balls, each spread out on the dirt field.

I admire him from afar as my sister approaches me.

She stands a few feet back when she says, "Oh, you've got it bad."

I scrunch my nose at her. "Do not! Okay, I totally do," I admit with a big smile. "But look at him!"

Matthew walks up to us. "What's up, Auntie?" He waves but keeps his distance.

I want to hug the big dude like I normally do and am sad when I can't.

I turn to Shelly. "Nikki didn't want to come?" I ask about my niece.

"Nah, she was happy outside drawing with chalk," Shelly replies.

Nick and his parents show up, and we all head to the baseball field.

Drew stands with his arms open wide. "Welcome to my practice à la quarantine."

I introduce all of them to Drew. Nick's parents show their appreciation and talk about Nick's goals, moving forward, while Matthew and Nick stare at him in awe. Their faces crack me up, and I'm getting a kick from just staring at them.

"Okay"—Drew slaps his hands together—"the number one goal here is that we keep our distance, which should be easy, playing baseball, but then I thought, *What about touching the ball?*" He picks up a ball and holds it up. "So, I have three different buckets here."

He points so we can see that one says *Drew*, the middle one says *Matthew*, and the third one says *Nick*.

"You are to only touch the balls in your bucket. Instead of throwing a ball back after you catch it, you just drop it to the ground next to you and pick up the ball from your bucket and throw that one instead. Does that make sense? So the other person's ball will only touch your glove and not your actual hand."

They both nod, and Nick's parents smile at the lengths he's gone to keep their son safe.

"Okay, you two go ahead and warm up. It's good mental practice too. You have to think every time to *not* touch the ball that was thrown to you. Baseball is a mental game, so this is an added bonus."

Drew continues to talk to Nick's parents as Shelly and I sit and watch. Drew's attention keeps turning to me, and every time he does, I can't hide the smile on my face.

"He is so stinking cute!" Shelly says. "Do you see how he keeps checking you out?"

I grin her way. "I know. It's been so unreal too. I've never gotten to know a guy like this. It's really forcing us to talk, you know?"

She laughs out loud. "Yeah, no sex to mess things up this way."

I groan. "That's the part that sucks. I want to touch him. Just once."

Her eyes widen. "You haven't even touched?"

"Nope." I shake my head sadly but then turn his way as I say, "His mom has a compromised immune system, so he's keeping his distance, and he's been getting very creative on ways to be together without being together."

"That's adorable. You know, I've always said you'll know how a guy feels by the effort he puts into getting to know you. I'd say, he's all in."

I smile at her as I shrug my shoulders and head toward him.

He sees me coming and steps away to talk to me.

"Thank you so much for doing this," I say.

"This is what I do. What I love. I'm excited you have a nephew who loves baseball." He reaches out his arm to touch me and pulls back with a sigh. "God, I'd love to just touch you, only for a second."

Chills run through my body as I take a shaky inhale.

"Sorry, I shouldn't have ..." He leaves it hanging in the air.

"No. You should have. The anticipation makes it more fun. We'll get there one day."

He winks. "Yeah, we will," he says before he runs off to the boys.

I watch as he takes the boys through multiple drills, showing them how to shuffle their feet, demonstrating how to stay in front of the ball, and even telling them tricks on how to keep the sun out of their face with a fly ball.

When he hits grounders to them, they field the balls with their gloves and then toss them to the side, straight from their gloves since he's hitting them balls from his bucket.

When they practice pitching, he pays extra attention to give them the same courtesy by not touching the balls they pick up. And after he throws balls to them for batting practice from his bucket, he tells them to go for a water break, and then he picks up the balls within the cages, all on his own.

Seeing him go the extra mile for kids he's never met is the cherry on top of this already-amazing man.

When the practice is over and the boys are exhausted, we all say good-bye.

When I go to do the same, he stops me. "Hey, Sharee?"

My sister nudges my arm before she grabs Matthew, and they keep heading toward their car.

I turn around. "Yeah?"

"Hang out a little. I thought I could show you some things too."

I laugh out loud. "Just because you got me to run doesn't mean I can hit a baseball."

"Don't doubt yourself. I bet you could," he says with a grin.

"Well"—I playfully slide toward him—"if I had you as a teacher," I say coyly.

He opens his arms to the sides. "I'm here, ready and willing."

"Willing, huh?"

"You have no idea," he says slowly and then tilts his head toward home plate. "Come on. I have a bat you can use that I haven't touched in weeks."

We go to where his stuff is, but I stay back to give him his space.

He grabs it by the barrel and hands it to me. "For you."

Day One

I take it and step back, giving it a good swing.

His eyes light up. "You're playing with me. You've done this before," he states.

"That would be a no, but I've been to enough games that I can tell how to swing."

"Then, let's see if you can hit." He steps back, moving closer to the pitching mound.

I hold the bat out and point it at him. "Don't laugh."

With hands up in surrender, he says, "Never."

He throws the ball, and I miss by a long shot, swinging around and almost falling on my ass.

He tries to hold back his laughter. "I'm impressed. You gave it your all for sure. Keep your eye on the ball."

"Easier said than done." I hold the bat up again, readying myself for the next pitch.

"Stick your butt out a tiny bit," he says.

"Like this?" I arch my back.

"A little more," he suggests, and I do. "Now, shake it just a little."

I start to and then stop. I stand up straight to face him. "Hey!"

He shrugs with a shit-eating grin. "Sorry, I had to. Okay, ready?" He holds up the ball.

I nod, and he throws it. I swing, and my hands sting when I hit the ball, sending it flying right back at him. He jumps and catches the ball just in time, so it doesn't hit him across the face.

"Whoa." He breathes out in disbelief. "Thank God I caught that. What would I have said to my new coach if I got injured?" he jokes. "*Sorry, Coach, but I couldn't catch the ball my girlfriend hit from the second pitch she'd ever had thrown at her, but, yeah, put me in on your infield, and I'll do just fine against the biggest guys.*"

He chuckles under his breath as I stand up, realizing what he said so very nonchalantly.

I tilt my head and grin when I ask, "Girlfriend?"

He smiles wide as he throws the ball up in the air only a few inches above himself before catching it again. "Yeah, girlfriend."

He winks, and I blow a kiss his way, wishing I could kiss him for real.

Day 12

April 7

My phone rings, and the normal excitement I feel is nothing compared to the mindfuck I'm watching on television right now.

"Oh. My. God. Please tell me you can turn on Netflix," I say to Drew, wasting no time.

"You too?" he says, exasperated knowing what's to come by the talk of the show that seems to be everywhere.

"Yes, and I'm taking you down with me. This *Tiger King* show is unreal. Just when I think it can't get any weirder, I start the next episode, and I was totally wrong! My mind is blown right now."

"That's what everyone is saying. I'm not really into watching some crazy guy with a mullet dance around with tigers."

I slap my hand on the couch. "I thought the same thing! Their marketing for this show is nothing compared to what it is." I press pause on my screen and sit up straighter, ready to fill him in.

I talk for twenty minutes, telling him all about Carole,

who has this cat sanctuary. She's literally doing the same thing these other two guys are, but she wants the other ones closed down and even has PETA on her side. But then I go on about how one zoo owner, Joe Exotic, has two husbands, and the other zoo owner, Doc, is basically running a harem of wives out of his zoo.

"Wait, what?" he asks, confused and as shocked as I am.

"Right?" I yell into the phone. "But then this Carole chick has a crazy past. Her husband, who was worth millions, suddenly disappeared twenty years ago, and they've never found his body. They think she killed him and fed him to the tigers!"

He laughs in disbelief into the phone. "This can't be real."

"That's the crazy part. It totally is! And now, this Joe Exotic guy is in jail because they say he hired someone to kill Carole."

"Did he?"

"I don't know! I'm only on episode three. You have to turn it on!"

"Hold on. Let me grab my computer," he says begrudgingly.

"Well, shoot. I know I filled you in, but you need to start from the top. Are you ready? Do you have water, snacks, everything you need? I promise you'll be sucked in."

He chuckles through the line. "I think I'll be fine."

I take a deep inhale. "You say that now. But don't say I didn't warn you," I tease and then think of what I just did. "Well, shoot, what am I to do now until you're caught up, so we can watch it together?"

"How are those runs coming? Is it time to jump back on the bandwagon?"

"Ugh! You would say that. Fine." I sigh. "The things I do for you," I say playfully.

"Go get 'em, girl. I'll be here, learning about your harem and tiger-feeding chick."

"Don't worry; you'll thank me later."

"Yeah, we'll see. Have a great run."

We hang up, and I regretfully close my laptop and head out for a run to pass the time until I can start the show back up.

Once I'm back from my run, I shower and grab some lunch. Then, I curl up on my couch and send Drew a text.

> Me: Are you finished yet?

> Drew: Don't bug me.

> Me: Ha! See, you're hooked.

> Drew: This show is like crack. Your description of it did it no justice.

I snort from laughing.

> Me: Then, hurry up.

> Drew: Then, stop texting. I keep having to press pause, so I don't miss anything.

I sit back on my couch and start scrolling through Facebook. Every *Tiger King* meme I see, I stop to read it.

When I see an update about a high school friend who has COVID-19 and is being moved out of ICU, I say a little prayer for him, so thankful he's doing well.

I check my county's daily update and learn there are only eighty-eight confirmed cases. I know that seems like a lot, but when it's compared to over a thousand in Santa Clara County and six hundred in San Francisco, we could have fared much worse.

New York is breaking my heart. My best friend lives there, and I check in with her daily as she stays home-bound. They have so many cases that I can't keep track of it anymore.

I'm searching for any news out of New York when I see the best thing ever. Every night at seven, the hospital workers change shifts, and everyone goes out on their balconies or windows, cheering for the people who are working tirelessly to help save their city.

The video I watch brings tears to my eyes. This is the America I love.

I find more stories about people coming together to support one another. Moms and daughters are making masks for everyone, and local restaurants are serving free meals to our first responders.

When I come across stories of crazies who literally cough and spit on produce or a man who even licked a bank door in Canada, I shake my head and sigh. I know this is a hard time, but people need to realize we're all in this together. Every single one of us is affected in some way or another.

I read about how some are saying there's a drug that's been around for years called hydroxychloroquine, which seems to be a game changer, but then I read about how others are saying the same drug isn't tested, so news anchors shouldn't be talking about it.

Just when I'm about to go further down the rabbit hole on the drug and its different reports, my text alert goes off.

Drew: You do know I hate you now, right?

Day One

I take a deep breath, ridding my mind of all the stories—scary, political, fearful, hopeful, and who knows what else—that I just read on the news sites and thank God for Drew and the distraction I've been craving. I smile big when I pick up the phone and call him.

"It's all your fault," he says.

I giggle. "I tried to warn you. You don't have to lie though. Deep down, you're thanking the shit out of me for making you watch it because it's the most addictive thing you've ever seen."

He sighs. "Fine, you win. I *need* to watch more. Did you see those wedding pictures from Carole and her new husband?"

I can't help the laugh that flies out of my mouth. "I forgot about that! What self-respecting man would do that?"

"Um, someone who knows she'll feed him to the tigers if he doesn't." He pauses. "Or she's really a dominatrix, and that's his leash."

"Oh my God! You're totally onto something there!"
We both laugh.

"Okay, are you ready to move on to episode four?"

"Yes!" I say, relieved that it's finally time. "I got lost in the hole that is the internet, looking up stuff about this virus."

He lets out a deep breath. "It's freaky out there."

"At least I found out a friend of mine is out of ICU, so that's great news."

"Yeah, that's awesome. A coach I had in the minor league a few years ago has it too. Last I heard, he was starting to feel better. It seems like a lot of people are fighting it and winning."

I nod, pressing my lips together. "I weird thought today."

"Do I want to know?" he deadpans, obviously teasing me.

It's nice to know he's getting to know me and my crazy ideas so well.

I chuckle. "Yes, you always want to know my thoughts because they're brilliant and forthcoming."

"Okay then, enlighten me, oh smart one."

"I saw that insurance companies are going to be reimbursing premiums on car insurance because no one is actually driving now. With no one driving, then car accidents are way down. Since they won't be paying out to fix those cars, they're giving people the money back to help them financially."

"Really? But then think about that. Auto body shops won't have cars to fix."

"Exactly. Things I didn't think about until we were forced to sit at home. But here's what really got me: if there are fewer accidents, that means less are dying on freeways. Did you know roughly thirty-seven thousand people are killed on freeways yearly?"

"Wow. No. That's a lot."

"Right? It breaks down to roughly a hundred a day. So, in a weird, twisted way, if we're on lockdown until May first, just in the month of April, three thousand lives that would have been lost in car accidents aren't going to happen. Well, hopefully. Some people are still on the road, so, you know ..."

"But many more are dying from the virus than three thousand."

I sigh. "I know. I was just trying to look for a silver lining. There's always something positive you can take out of a negative situation; you just have to find it."

"Like me meeting you," he says breathlessly.

"Like me meeting you," I say, matching his tone with a grin on my face.

"Okay, my silver-lining girl, let's forget about the world's troubles and get lost in the troubles of three other crazy lives that I didn't even know existed until a few hours ago."

I smile. "Let's do this." I press my lips together and then twist them before asking, "Do you think I could ever get you to—"

"Don't even think about it," he interrupts me.

"But you don't even know what I was going to say!"

"I know! But if it has anything to do with this show, then the answer is no. Hell no actually." He laughs.

"Fine. But remember, I got you to watch the show."

"Yeah, I have a feeling I'm going to be giving in a lot when it comes to you."

I gasp. "You say that like it's a bad thing."

"Believe me, it's not. It's a very, very good thing. Now, shut up and press play."

"Bossy, bossy," I tease.

"And you love it," he says, and I wish I could see his face right now.

I bet, if we were in front of each other, he would have winked at me, making me all mushy inside.

I smile as I respond, "I do."

Day 13

April 8

I'm watching the president's daily briefing when I start cracking up and immediately pick up the phone to call Drew.

"Hey there," he says, instantly melting my heart.

"Are you watching?" I ask once I recover.

"Not again ..." he whines. "You can't get me addicted to another crazy show. *Tiger King* was enough for a lifetime of mindfuckery."

"Ha-ha-ha. Don't even lie. You were just as drawn into it as I was! But no, I meant, are you watching the president's daily briefing?"

"Oh shit. Is everything okay? What happened? Are we under attack or something?" He panics, and I can tell he's getting up to turn on the television.

"No, silly! Nothing like that. But a reporter asked if the president would consider pardoning Joe Exotic!"

"He did not ..." he says in disbelief.

"Oh, yes, he did!" I chuckle. "I guess one of his sons made a comment that he was on Joe's side, so the reporter wondered if the president was too."

Day One

"We're in a pandemic that's literally shutting down our entire world, and someone thought it was a good idea to ask that?"

"See! Everyone is addicted to this show."

"Yeah, but come on. Please don't tell me Trump went along with the question."

"No." I sigh. "He said he wasn't familiar with the show, so he didn't know the full story."

"Thank God!"

"Oh, stop." I giggle.

"What else are you doing with your day?"

"You'd be so proud of me! I fixed my sink all on my own." I hold my head up high with a big smile even though no one's around to see me.

"Look at you! What was wrong?"

"It was clogged. I took apart the U-thing under the sink, and when that didn't work, I snaked out the line."

"You? Snaked out the line?" he asks in shock.

" 'What, like it's hard?' " I state in my best Elle Woods voice from *Legally Blonde*.

He chuckles, so he must get my movie reference. "I'm impressed, is all. I didn't know I was dating such a do-it-herselfer."

"There's a lot you don't know about me," I taunt.

"Yes, and I can't wait to change that."

Chills run through my body and lust pools in my stomach as I take a deep breath when all the ways he can learn about me swarm my thoughts.

"So, what are we watching tonight?" he asks.

The thought of sitting on the phone with him again breaks my heart. I want him closer. I want to be able to sneak glances at him when he's not looking. I want to hear him breathe or smell his cologne even if it's across the room.

A thought comes to my mind. "How about you come here?"

"Um ..." I hear the hesitation in his voice.

"I'll make us a picnic in my front yard."

"A picnic?"

"Yeah. Only for dinner instead of lunch."

"Sounds perfect. What time?"

"How's seven?"

"I'll see you then."

It took time to figure out what to make us for dinner. Since this is the first time he's going to try my cooking, I want it to be my best, but what if my best isn't something he likes? The stress is for real. Then, add on not wanting to go to the store if I didn't have to, and I was a ball of frustration.

After trying to put together four different meals, all missing one ingredient that was vital, I settled on lasagna after I found some ground beef in the freezer.

I've heard people say they slave over lasagna, but I have a recipe that is to die for and surprisingly easy to make with the no-boil noodles.

Once I'm ready to put it in the oven, I race to the shower to finish getting ready while it cooks. I spend my time picking out the perfect outfit that is both cute and comfy since we'll be sitting on my grass in the front yard.

Before our food is ready, I remove silverware and a plate from the dishwasher, holding a clean towel to grab each item and setting it aside, being careful to not touch anything he will be using.

My text goes off with the familiar baseball-hitting sound just as I take the lasagna out of the oven.

Drew: I'll bring wine. Red or white?

Day One

Me: Great! Red for sure.

I snap a picture and send it his way.

Drew: I'm literally drooling right now. Lasagna is my favorite. How'd you know? ;-)

Me: Good guess. See you soon!

I head outside and set up our makeshift picnic in my front yard. With two blankets, I place his spot and then mine, keeping them spread apart. Next to each blanket, I place boxes that I stuff with books to give us each a little table to eat our dinner on.

As he pulls up, I stand and hold out my hands, showing off the work I've done.

"Well, aren't you cute?" he says as he exits his car.

"I even made our little tables more stable with books." I lean on them to show how they won't collapse.

"I meant, *you*." He grins. "But, yes, this all looks great as well."

I try to hide the blush his words caused before turning and saying, "I'll go get the food."

I swear I hear him chuckle at my awkwardness. When I turn around, I see him checking me out.

"You like what you see?" I ask coyly.

"You have no idea."

I grin and continue my way to the house. When I come back, he's sitting on his blanket with two glasses of wine already poured.

I set the lasagna down with a proud expression.

"That smells amazing," he says.

"Wait until you try it. Now, I made sure to take your plate, silverware, and glass straight out of the dishwasher, holding them only by a clean towel so I didn't touch anything and—"

"You didn't have to go through all that trouble," he says.

I can tell he wants to reach out to touch me to make sure his words are meaningful, but he holds back and grins instead.

I shrug. "I just wanted to make sure you knew I was taking this seriously. I know you have a reason to worry about it, so I am too."

He smiles bigger, and I look down, grabbing the spatula to cut him a piece.

"Now, how much do you want?" I place my tool on top of the lasagna, asking him with my eyes where I should cut the food.

"Right there is good," he says.

"Obviously, there's plenty, so you can always come back for more too. Here, hold out your plate."

He does, and I dish him up before getting mine. We both sit at our spots a few feet away and eat our dinner.

"Have you seen how bands are doing covers of other bands' songs and posting them to Instagram?" I ask.

He shakes his head after he takes a bite and wipes his mouth with his napkin. "No. Any you like?"

"Yes!" I say dramatically. "Jen Ledger from Skillet did a cover of 'Gravity' by Papa Roach with a band called From Ashes to New. It. Was. Amazing! I shared it to my stories, so you can check it out later."

"What makes you think I've viewed your stories?" he teases.

"Don't lie. You have totally been checking me out. You do realize that accidental heart you gave on a photo from a year ago still notified me even though you took it off really quick, right?" I say with a smirk.

"Busted," he replies playfully. "Then, you've been checking me out too?"

"Uh, duh! I've seen everything. Your Facebook, Twitter, YouTube, ESPN, MLB Network—"

"Okay, okay, not fair. You have more avenues to cyber-stalk."

"Yep, sure do. Don't be jealous. Sorry I'm not as famous as you are."

He takes an extra napkin I have sitting between us, crumples it, and throws it at me.

I laugh and dodge the object just in time. "And you say you're a baseball player." I make a *tsk-tsk* sound with my tongue.

Once we're done with our dinner, I bring everything inside as the sun starts to go down. When I come back, he's lying on his back, staring up at the stars starting to shine through.

I take a moment to check him out before making my presence known. His interest in the stars is obvious. He even lifts his arm like he's measuring something between the tips of his fingers.

"Are you a star buff?" I ask as I make my way back to my blanket.

"I've always been fascinated by them. Don't know a ton though. I try to find the Big Dipper and stuff like that. I wish I knew more. How about you?"

I lie down and stare up at the vast sky. "Me too. I took a few classes in college though."

"Then, what's that?" he asks, pointing to five stars that make a *W* image.

"That's Cassiopeia. Greek mythology says she thought she was the most beautiful thing around, so she was placed in the sky as a punishment. The *W* makes up her crown."

"Yeah, I've heard that name before."

I show him a few other things as we take in the night sky.

As the darkness surrounds us, he turns his head, so he's looking at me instead of the sky. He reaches in his pocket and pulls out a tiny bottle of hand sanitizer. Squirting some on his hand, he lays his arm out flat toward me.

"Give me your hand," he says.

Our eyes meet, and my chest tightens. When I reach out, he rubs the sanitizer between our fingers and then keeps them there, holding my hand as both of our arms are stretched out. We're keeping our distance yet touching each other for the first time.

Feeling him sends a zing through my body. His hand is warm, and I can feel the slight callus he has from swinging a bat.

I keep my sight glued on his.

I want so badly to touch him more.

I want to feel his lips and know what they taste like.

I inhale a deep breath as we stay like this. For now, I'll take all I can get. For now, this is our own version of being *alone together*, just like the hashtag keeps saying.

Day 14

April 9

It's a damn good thing I fixed my sink because I went to run my dishwasher and realized I had zero soap. When I thought about running to the store, I had to be real with myself. If I were to get this virus just because I was too lazy to wash these dishes by hand, I'd never forgive myself.

So, instead of running to the store, I blast some music and go to town on washing an entire load of dishes by hand. When I think about how most of these are dirty because I made dinner for Drew last night, it makes it all worth it.

Once I'm done, I curl up on my couch with a cup of coffee and turn on the TV. Scrolling through the channels, I see MLB Network is replaying the 1977 World Series and turn it on just for the laugh.

When I see *SportsCenter* is airing still, I click on it, wondering how they're running the show now and if it's broadcast live or through Zoom and people's houses.

I'm not lost on the fact that I turned on *SportsCen-ter*—a show that I've only seen when my sister's husband has it on at their place. And, yes, it's all Drew's fault.

The show is breaking news of an NFL team trading some guy named Brandin Cooks and a future pick to the Texans for a second-round pick, and within seconds, I'm lost on who's who and what team they're referencing.

I go to change the channel when they tease the upcoming touching story about the newly signed San Francisco Giants player Andrew Miller.

My eyes bug out of my head as I sit up straighter, almost spilling my coffee. I grab my phone, thinking I should call Drew to tell him, and then I pause and want to smack myself in the head. Obviously, if there's a touching story about him, he knows about it.

Then, a small pang hits me in my chest. *If he knew about it, then why didn't he tell me?*

I wait—not so patiently, I might add—for the show to come back on. When it does, the host introduces an organization called More Than Baseball. Their spokesman tells us about the minor league and how things work behind the scenes. I've always thought if you're a baseball player, you make money. Boy, was I wrong.

They talk about all the different levels before you get to the majors and how some of these guys make as little as one hundred dollars a week. My mind is blown. They have to travel all over the country for days at a time. *How can they possibly hold down another job as well?*

They also mention how the players have to provide all of their own equipment and housing. When the spokesman said there are players who are hungry and sleeping on air mattresses, only to wake up and play for thousands of paying customers, it breaks my heart.

Included are stories of Adam Wainwright, a veteran St. Louis pitcher, and his wife donating two hundred fifty thousand dollars to Cardinals minor leaguers and the Colorado Rockies player Daniel Murphy donating one hundred thousand dollars in the past few days to the organization.

I'm so engrossed in their conversation that I totally forgot that Drew was coming on until they split the screen and welcome him to the discussion.

Seeing him on-screen melts my heart in ways I didn't know possible. Every day, I feel more for this man, and just the sight of him brings those emotions deeper.

"We want to welcome Andrew Miller to the show, who is the newest San Francisco Giants first baseman. Thanks for joining us, Andrew."

"Thanks for having me," Drew says.

"I hear you were a recipient of More Than Baseball's program. Can you tell us more about that?" the host asks.

Drew starts with a slight chuckle. "*Recipient* is probably not the right word. I wouldn't be here if it wasn't for More Than Baseball. I was that guy who was sleeping on an air mattress after each game. I had to make my way up through the ranks of Single-A to where I am now. I didn't go to a fancy college or get drafted right away. I started at the bottom, and to say it was a struggle is a bit of an understatement."

"Did you really not have a normal bed?" the host asks.

Drew runs his hand down his face like he's embarrassed and doesn't believe he's saying this all on national television.

He lets out a deep breath and continues, "I was lucky that I was moving up through the ranks pretty fast, but that meant, I had to move a lot. It was easier to throw my mattress in a box because I couldn't afford the big trucks every time I moved. My mom was battling cancer during my time in the minors, so I wouldn't dare to ask my parents for money."

"How's your mom now?" the host asks, obviously concerned.

Drew's face lights up. "She's great. In remission now. Thanks for asking."

"Glad to hear it. So, how did More Than Baseball help you, and why did you donate one hundred thousand dollars to the organization?" the host asks.

My mouth falls to the floor as I blink my eyes wide. *Did he just say one hundred thousand dollars?*

Drew grins from ear to ear. "My life changed once someone introduced me to More Than Baseball. I was able to get help with buying food, living a normal life, and they gave me hope. I barely had my contract signed before the pandemic happened. If the lockdown had happened a month later, I'd have been back with all my friends, making four hundred dollars a week. It just didn't seem right. I had a signing bonus that was supposed to be the down payment on my new apartment, but the shelter-in-place order here in California made that purchase fall through just the other day, so I figured there was no better place for the money to go. I'm lucky enough that my parents live close to San Francisco, so I'm staying with them. I know there are a few guys who aren't so lucky and could really use the help."

"So, you're bringing the program full circle?" the host asks.

"Exactly." Drew nods.

"Well, I'm sure the players who will benefit from your generosity will appreciate it. Thanks for coming on."

"Thanks for having me," Drew says.

His window closes, and the host fills the screen.

"There you have it. From veterans of the game to their newest players, everyone in the baseball family is helping one another."

I have to wipe the tears from my eyes that kept popping up as Drew spoke. He went through all of that while his mom was fighting cancer, and I'm sure it was very hard. Knowing he was able to make it this far proves the fight he has in him.

Day One

He's a determined man, and it makes him even sexier than I thought before. Both inside and out.

I pick up the phone and dial him right away.

"Hey there, cutie," he says like he's been chilling, watching a movie, and not giving a huge interview.

"Drew …" I say, trying to hold back the tears again.

"You saw, didn't you?" he says, and I can't tell if that's a good thing or a bad thing.

"I did. I'm just blown away. Why didn't you tell me?"

He laughs nervously. "Which part?"

"All of it. Your struggles. Your place falling through. Donating the money …"

He sighs. "I didn't do it for the recognition. When they asked me to do the interview this morning, I originally said no, but the guys from More Than Baseball said it would have more of an impact for the organization."

"It so did. You did great." He's silent, and I can tell he's uncomfortable with the attention it brought, so I change the subject. "Then, tell me about your place."

"I was purchasing an apartment in the city. When the shelter in place started happening, the people I was buying it from lost their jobs and pulled out of the deal. It was technically too late to do so, but I couldn't take their home from them, so we canceled it on both ends with no big deal."

"Will you find another place?"

"Who knows? Maybe I wasn't supposed to live in the city. I mean, you're here, so …"

"Drew …" I say, tears filling my eyes again, but I try to hide them.

"Is that weird? Did I just scare the shit out of you? I mean, fuck, I guess it has only been a few days. Maybe I'm just jumping to conclusions. There are always places I can find there."

"Hell no, you won't." I laugh. "Like you said, I'm here,

and, yes, we definitely need to see where this goes before you go off and buy a place too far away from me."

He laughs, and I can hear the relief in his voice. "You know, dating a baseball player isn't easy. I'll be on the road a lot."

"And I don't work over the summer. So, who knows? You might open your hotel room to find a naked girl sprawled on your bed, waiting to thank her favorite player for giving her such a great show on the field."

"Sprawled on the bed, huh? Are you trying to kill me right now?"

"Nah, just trying to give you visuals for your spank bank when you go to bed tonight."

His voice comes out as a growl. "You are. You're trying to kill me. I knew it."

"It will all be worth it. I promise," I say with the cheesiest grin on my face, glad he can't see me.

"Believe me, I have no doubt."

Day 15

April 10

A knock on my door shocks the hell out of me. I reach for my phone and check my Ring app. As it comes on, I see a delivery vehicle parked in my driveway and a guy taking a picture of whatever he left on my porch before walking away.

Since I didn't order anything, I approach the door with caution, as you can never be too careful these days.

Wait, who am I kidding? I can see on my app that no one is there anymore.

I open the door and see a very large box. I lean down to pick it up, figuring it's going to be heavy, and I almost topple over when I give it way too much effort and find out it's only a pound or two.

Questioning it even more now, I take it inside—after I've wiped it down, of course, with the Clorox wipe I grabbed from my entryway.

After I open the box, I'm even more confused when I see a pillow inside. I close the lid again and check to see if it was delivered to the wrong house. When I verify that it is indeed my address and name printed on the label, I open it again and pull the pillow out.

To my surprise, the thing keeps coming and coming, and I have to stand up straight to get it all the way out of the box. I hold it up to see it's a body pillow.

I definitely did not order this.

The order form is in the bottom of the box, and when I flip it over, I see it's from Drew.

As I walk back to my couch, I think about what to say to him.

Um, thanks for the body pillow. Can I ask why you sent it to me though?

Would that be rude?

I click his name, which is now on the top of my Favorites screen, and wait for him to answer.

"Did it arrive?" he says.

I let out a laugh. "So, you did in fact send me a package?" I ask, wondering if maybe he ordered the wrong thing.

"You don't like it?" His voice sounds a little hurt.

"Um, I think they sent me the wrong item."

"Oh no. Really? Jeez, how can you possibly mess up a body pillow? It's not like there are similar things. It's a really big—"

"So, you meant to send me that? Because that's what I got," I say, a little confused.

He laughs out loud. "Yes, I meant to send you a body pillow."

"Uh, can I ask why?" I try to sound happy but still uncertain.

"Since I can't be there to cuddle up with you tonight when we watch a movie, I wanted you to cuddle up with the pillow and pretend it's me." His voice is uplifting and adorable.

I can't help the giggle that escapes my lips.

Day One

"It's lame. I'm sorry." He sighs.

"No! Oh my God, it's the cutest thing ever." I unwrap the plastic wrap from the pillow and curl up with it on my couch. "It's my own personal Drew. And it's something I'll be able to use, even after this quarantine is over and when you're gone for away games."

"Exactly!" he says, proud of himself and his idea.

"I think I'll take the pillowcase to my friend who has this machine that prints pictures on fabric. I can have your face printed on it and lie with you at night."

"Okay, now, you're getting weird." He laughs, and I can tell he's being playful.

"Hell no! I want my Drew pillow. You're the one who put the idea in my head. If you haven't found out yet, I'm an all-in type of girl."

"Yeah, I can tell. But it might be freaky, sleeping next to a blown-up picture of myself."

"What if I hide it until you're gone?"

He laughs. "I'd still know it existed. What if someone saw it and we had to explain?"

He can barely hold in his laughter at our ridiculous conversation, but I love that he plays along with my crazy ideas.

"Hmm ... okay, that might be weird. People might think I dry-hump the pillow when you're gone."

His laughter radiates through the phone, and my cheeks start to hurt from smiling so big.

"What if I have the Giants logo and the number twenty-four printed on it with Miller somewhere?" I ask.

He thinks about it. "Okay ... I'll agree to that. That would be cool. I can see that lying across the back of our bed. Yeah, I'd like that actually."

"Our bed?" I ask in surprise.

"Hey, you're the one who just said you're an all-in type of girl. I'm just following your lead."

I sigh kiddingly. "Hmm, I did say that, didn't I?"

"Why, yes, you did."

I lean back on my new pillow, pretending it's him, and then ask, "How tall are you again?"

"About six-two. Why?"

"I'm trying to envision what it would be like to cuddle next to you."

He lets out a breath. "We'll know for real here … someday … hopefully."

"How long do you think this will last? I've heard so many different reports that I think my head's going to explode. They announced already that school wouldn't be going back at all. I don't understand how they can say that this early. I mean, we still have the rest of April, all of May, and the first week of June. That's eight more weeks before school was supposed to be out." I stop and sigh.

Eight weeks. Will Drew and I be like this for eight more weeks?

I saw on TV that the MLB is talking about quarantining all the baseball players in one place down in Arizona or Florida, so they can play to empty stadiums. If that happens, he'd have to leave right away. I'd never get a chance to know what his arms felt like, wrapped around me. I'd never even get a chance to kiss him before he left.

My chest aches at the thought.

"Hey, what's going on in that head of yours?" he asks.

"Sorry. I have these moments of disbelief sometimes. Like, I have to stop myself and ask if this is really happening."

"I know. I feel the same way. I think everyone is feeling that way though. I promise you, you're not alone."

I let out a sarcastic laugh. "Well, actually, yeah, I am alone. Wait, not now, now that I have my Drew pillow!"

He sighs. "You'll never be alone with me in the picture now."

Day One

"I did hear today that they think we've hit the peak. That's good news, right?"

"It's very good news. So, maybe this May first date will actually happen."

"May first ..." I say more to myself than to him. "So, that's twenty more days."

"Yep ... twenty more days."

We sit in silence as we let that set in.

"Hey, do me a favor," I ask.

"Anything."

"Do you have a measuring tape?"

"I'm sure my dad does. Why?"

"Go get it, please. I want you to measure something for me."

I hear him rustle around and stand up. He walks through his house, and I hear his parents ask if he's talking to me.

When he responds, "Of course," my heart does a happy dance.

I can hear his mom in the background say, "Tell her hello for us," and I dance even more.

It's like they've already welcomed me into their family, and the calmness that washes over me is unlike anything I've ever felt before. Maybe he's right. With him around, I'll never be alone.

The sound changes slightly when he enters the garage, like there's an echo around him. "Okay, I have the measuring tape. What am I doing with it?"

"Pull out five feet five inches," I direct.

"Five feet and five inches," he says under his breath as I hear the movement of the tape in the background. "Okay, got it. Now what?"

"Hold it up against your body and tell me where it comes to on you."

"The very top is right below my shoulder. Why?"

I let out a content breath. "It's perfect."

"What is?"

"I'll fit right in the flat part of your chest, and you'll be able to wrap your arms around me without having to bend down or lift your arms at a weird angle."

I close my eyes and imagine what that would feel like. His warmth pressed against me as I wrap my arms around his waist. Or even better, I'd bring my arms in against my body, placing my hands under my chin, and let him hold me completely.

"You really would fit perfectly," he says, and I can tell it's genuine.

"I can't wait to feel it for real," I say.

"Me too. I promise it won't be the twenty days."

"Yeah?" I ask.

"Yeah. I don't think I can wait that much longer," he says with a chuckle.

" 'You don't love me; you just love my doggy-style,' " I say, all dramatic-like.

The laugh that escapes his lips echoes around him even more since he's still in the garage, and I crack up along with him.

Only time will tell.

Day 16

April 11

My face is flushed, and my pulse is starting to race when my phone rings. The familiar clapping of "Centerfield" by John Fogerty turns my face even warmer.

I slam the paperback book I was reading down on the couch and take a deep breath. My mind was already racing, my desires building out of control.

Jeannine, my friend in New York, sent me a book—*Black Widow* by Lauren Runow—that she said was her favorite by this author. I had known she read dirty books, but holy hell, this book is going to make my little predicament with Drew even harder.

No, I'm not a sexual deviant, and I've never met guys on Tinder for a quick fuck, so I should be used to going a long time without sex, but now that I have Drew around, it's been even harder.

It's like a Girl Scouts Thin Mint cookie. You don't crave them year-round, but when they're around, you want to devour the entire box over and over and over again. Thin Mints are always the first to sell out, and this is why.

Drew has become my Thin Mint, and it really sucks, knowing he's right there, staring at me to attack him, and I can't. This is worse than any diet I've ever been on.

I close my eyes and swipe to answer the phone call.

"Hello?" I say, mad my voice didn't sound as level as I'd hoped.

"Hey. What's going on?" he says.

I try to hide my laugh, wondering if I should tell him what's really going on.

Oh, you know, I'm over here, thinking about masturbating to a really dirty book. How about you?

I go for nonchalant instead. "Just reading a book."

"Anything good?"

"My friend recommended it, so I'm thinking it will be."

"What's it about?"

The laugh escapes my lips, and I decide, *What the hell?* So, I go for it.

I cover my face with my hand as I whisper, "A sex club."

"Oh," he drawls. "You read dirty books. Man, I'm seeing a whole new side of you."

"Hey! It's contemporary romance. And, yes, most couples—minus us right now—have sex. So, yes, it explains the sex but—"

"Whoa, no judgment here," he cuts me off. "And believe me, we will rectify our little issue very soon."

I can't help but giggle. "Our issue?"

"Yes, because, right now, it's an issue. A huge issue. And, um"—he pauses, and I can hear him rustling around—"it's getting bigger, the more we talk about it."

I let out a sharp laugh. "Do you have a growing problem over there?"

"Oh no problems in that department. Only problem I have is that you're there while I'm here."

I sigh. "Yeah, I'm definitely here. All alone."

"Why don't you read me something from that little

Day One

book you have there since you don't have to worry about anyone around you hearing?"

My eyes widen. *Can I really do that?*

"Um, I'm not ..."

"What? You've never had phone sex before?" His voice drops an octave, making my mouth water.

"From reading a book? No." I giggle some more.

"Have you ever done it at all?"

I exhale and admit, "No."

"Even better. Why don't you read me something dirty?"

"Well, I was getting to a scene when the phone rang actually."

"See, it's like I knew your brain was saying, *Gosh, I wish I could fuck Drew right now.*"

A sharp inhale enters my chest as my core tightens.

"Nice to know I hit the mark," he says. "Now, tell me what happened up until the part you're at?"

"There's a girl, Kamii, who lost her husband and has become a bit of a workaholic. She meets a girl named Becca, who is this outgoing, crazy girl, and she wants to bring Kamii out of her shell. I just got to the part where Becca is taking Kamii to the club for the first time."

"And what kind of club is it again?" he asks, and I can tell he's trying to get me to say it.

"A sex club," I say and then decide if we're going to do this, I'm jumping all in. "But even better ... it's an anonymous sex club."

"Anonymous?"

"Yes. They don't use real names, and they wear masks, so it's supposed to be sex with strangers. It's based out of San Francisco too. Maybe we can look for one when all of this is over ..."

"Are you serious?" he asks, surprised.

I laugh out loud. "Um, no. Don't get your hopes up on that one, big boy."

"That's okay. I'm sure we won't need other people to keep us happy. I'll keep you satisfied."

"Oh, really? Confident much?"

"Very. Now, read."

"Yes, sir." I laugh before inhaling a breath, and then I start to read.

I sit quietly, shocked at where I am, hoping I don't look like the most prudish virgin, sitting here by myself.

I'm both very thankful and extremely upset with this rule telling me I can't join in. Then, I wonder, How is it that I can be both upset and thankful for the same rule? *If there wasn't this rule, could I really just walk up like Becca did and join them?*

The answer is no. I couldn't. I'd never have the guts to do that. *The thought saddens me more than I'd like to admit.*

What am I even doing here?

I bring my fingertips to my mouth and start to slightly tug on my lower lip when I suddenly feel the heat from someone sitting next to me. When I turn, I see it's him. Eros. And he's alone, next to me.

Where did the other woman go?

I drop my fingers from my lips and start to play with the straw in my drink, looking forward, watching the show unfolding in front of me.

There are three guys and three girls. Two of the girls have been stripped of their clothes and are starting in on one of the man's clothes. Becca is lying down on the bed. One man is stripping her clothes while she already has another man's dick in her mouth. She's up on her elbow, leaning to the side, working his dick between her lips, as the other man finishes taking off her skirt.

She's completely naked now, and the man leans in, licking her folds. The familiar ache between my legs heightens

Day One

I can't believe what I'm seeing. Right in front of me.

"And I can't believe you were actually reading this," Drew interrupts with a laugh. "I knew you were my dream girl, but damn, you just upped that to a level I hadn't known existed."

"Dream girl?" I ask breathlessly.

"Very much so. Now, keep reading."

I reposition myself before I begin again. Reading this and then hearing him call me his dream girl are doing some crazy things to my insides. I'm dying to touch myself, but I fight it off as I continue.

I close my legs tightly, shifting in my seat, trying to ease the need I feel.

Heat starts to overwhelm my body, and I realize it's Eros; he's sliding closer to me, pushing his body against mine. A shy smile slips from my lips before I turn my attention back to the scene.

Becca is still on her back, but now, a female is straddling her face, and the guy who was licking her before is now doing her slowly as he watches her devour the female. My vision locks on him as he slowly pushes himself in and out of her while she licks the woman she doesn't even know.

I'm shocked.

I'm mortified.

I'm more turned on than I have ever been in my entire life.

"Yeah, right there with her right now. How is that even possible?" Drew asks. "Please tell me you are too."

I let out a shaky breath, not able to answer him.

"Yeah, you are. What happens next?"

I continue.

My chest is tight, and my stomach starts to ache as my breathing gets so erratic that I can't hide it anymore.

To change my focus and try to calm down, I look around the scene to see the other two guys with one girl. They're sitting on a couch with the girl bouncing up and down on one guy while sucking on the other, who is standing next to them. He's leaning down, rubbing her breasts, as the other guy rubs her clit.

I hear her moan in ecstasy around the guy's dick, and I feel myself get wetter than I ever thought was possible from just watching people.

I can't just sit here. I have to do something.

The glass I was holding is still in my hands, so I open my legs only wide enough to slide the glass down between my thighs, suddenly very thankful Becca made me wear this short skirt. The feeling of the cold glass up against my soaked panties is pushing me further than I imagined. The coldness along with the hardness of the glass pressed against me causes my clit to tingle, releasing pure ecstasy.

Slowly, I move my hips from side to side, trying to hide my movements and not make what I'm doing obvious to anyone around. With my vision stuck on the body of a woman I don't know while a man's dick slides in and out of her, I feel myself start to almost drool from my slightly parted lips.

I think I'm getting away with my own private little scene until Eros slides closer, and I hear him whisper in my ear, "Let me help you."

"Fuck me, Sharee. I'm so fucking hard right now. I don't know if you should continue," Drew says, his voice laced with pain.

I take a breath before letting it out. "I wish I could help you."

"Help me?"

I bite my lip and nod even though I know he can't see me.

Day One

"How would you like to help me, Sharee?"

The way he says my name pushes me over the edge. I put the book down and get more comfortable on my couch. And by more comfortable, I mean, I run my fingers down my stomach and in between my legs.

"I want to feel how big your cock is," I say as I drop my head back on the couch and rub myself through my pajama pants.

"I wish you could. I don't remember the last time I was so hard. It's been like torture ever since I met you."

"Have you been jacking off to thoughts of me?" I ask.

"Every day," he says breathlessly. "It's like a dream to do it right now, hearing your voice."

A groan escapes his lips, and visions of him sliding his hand down his cock makes my chest tight.

"Please tell me you're touching yourself," he says.

"Yes," I whisper.

"Are you on the outside or inside of your clothes?"

"Outside."

"If I tell you what to do, will you do it?"

I nod, humming into the phone as my response.

"Close your eyes and envision it's my hand as you move up to your stomach, slowly touching the top of your panty line before slipping underneath the fabric, all the way until you feel your slit."

As my fingers glide over the smooth skin, I feel the wetness against my fingertips.

"Move your fingers around until you reach your clit."

A little squeak escapes my lips, and he moans when he hears I've hit my mark.

"Fuck, I've wondered what sounds you would make. That's going to be ingrained in my brain for the rest of my life."

He takes a deep inhale, and all I can think of is him holding back his urge as he moves his hand up and down his shaft.

"Now, play with your clit, twirl around on it before sliding down and slipping one finger inside. As soon as it's all the way in, I want you to slide it all the way out. Repeat that motion until I say to stop."

I spread my legs wider as I do as he said, imagining it's him controlling my body right now.

"Continue to do so while cupping your hand around the mound of your pussy, giving it pressure on your clit."

I do, and a loud moan escapes my lips. He growls in return.

"Keep your pressure there as you insert another finger and start moving both of them in and out, only slightly, keeping them inside you."

"Yeah," I say breathlessly.

"You like that?" he asks, his voice cracking.

"Yes, Drew. Very much."

"God, I love my name on your lips. Say it again."

"Drew. Drew. Oh my God, Drew," I say as my body starts to tingle and burn in all the right places.

"Are you close?"

"Yes, Drew. So close."

"Now, put your fingers deep inside you and flick them back and forth, keeping pressure on your clit."

I moan so loud that I should be embarrassed, but I'm not. I'm flying so high, climbing and climbing some more.

"Yes, Sharee. Right there. Are you ready? Come with me," he says more as a grunt.

I topple over, coming hard around my fingers. My entire body freezes, and I ride the waves rolling through me.

My head falls back, I drop my phone, and my eyes clench shut as I find my breath again. When I do, I can't help but laugh as I realize what just happened. Once I've come completely down, I grab the phone and bring it back up to my ear.

"Did we just ..." I ask in disbelief.

Day One

"Fuck yeah, we did. If the real thing is anything like that, I'm in trouble."

I laugh. "Yeah, me too."

"So, you felt that?"

"In my toes? Oh, yeah."

"You're my girl, Sharee. This. Us. I'm sold."

"And you haven't even kissed me yet," I say with a giggle.

"I don't need to. They always say, when you meet the one, you just know. I never understood that. But now, especially after that, I know."

"Me too," I say, trying to fight the tears filling my eyes.

"We got this. We can do this. We met during this quarantine because someone up there knew we would make it through. I have no doubt now. I can't fucking wait to do that for real."

I laugh. "Many, many times."

"Many times for sure." He chuckles. "Go get cleaned up and call me right back. You can curl up with my pillow, and we'll watch a movie together."

I agree and hang up the phone.

Before I stand, I smile in absolute disbelief. I've definitely met the man I'm going to marry. The worst time of my life is turning into the best.

Day 17

April 12

It's Easter, yet in the little bubble I currently live in, you wouldn't know it. Every Easter, my sister and I normally make the trek back to our mom's house to have dinner together and hang out. I dye eggs with her kids, and she enjoys the time, not having to worry about the mess her kids are making.

It is always a fun, simple day; looking back on it, I realize I took it for granted. Whoever thought something as normal as hanging out with family would be taken away from us?

I thought about still dyeing eggs, but right now, I kind of want to save my eggs for breakfast for the next week, so I don't have to go to the store. I guess a tradition takes on a different meaning now.

Both my mom and dad called, and I talked to Shelly, too, but otherwise, my day has been spent watching *E:60* on ESPN. Who knew ESPN had such touching stories that could bring you to tears?

When I see *The Notebook* is on a different station, I

Day One

curl up even more and settle in for the good cry I know is coming my way.

During the movie, my Ring app keeps going off. Since I can hear the kids from across the street outside on their bikes, having Easter egg hunts, I ignore it and continue to watch the movie.

Halfway through, I hear a knock on my front door. After pressing pause on the movie, I hop up and head to the door, thinking one of the kids threw a ball over my fence.

When I open it, I see Drew standing on my sidewalk with his favorite hat on, slacks, a dress shirt, and a smile.

Not jumping into his arms is much harder than I thought it would be after last night. I have to hold my hands together in front of me to stop myself from doing so.

"Look at you, all dressed up," I say.

He glances down with a smirk. "Mom still made Easter dinner, and she wanted me to bring you some."

I smile as I cover my heart with my hand. "She's so sweet. I wish I could have you come in."

He shrugs. "It's okay. I have something for you. Come here."

He steps off my porch, and when I come outside to join him, I see my entire driveway is decorated in an elaborate design, colored with chalk.

I squeal in surprise. "Did you do this?"

I turn to him, and his face is covered in the biggest, proudest smile.

"Happy Easter," he says.

"I didn't know you were an artist."

He shrugs. "It's just for fun."

"For fun? Oh my God."

I stop to take in the entire drawing of flowers, eggs, and even a bunny. *Happy Easter* is written across the center.

I check out his clothes and then his hands. "How is chalk not everywhere?"

He chuckles under his breath. "I changed my clothes in the car before I knocked on your door."

"You had this nice outfit in your car?"

He nods like it's no big deal as he glances down at what he's wearing. "Yeah, it's Easter. I didn't want to show up in torn jeans and covered in dust. I was so worried you'd come outside and ruin the surprise too. Glad I was able to finish."

"You can thank *The Notebook* for being on TV. When my Ring kept going off, I thought it was the kids," I say, pointing across the street.

They all come running as their mom yells to make sure they keep their distance from us.

"It turned out so cool!" one of the girls says.

"How long did it take you?" I ask.

"A little over an hour," Drew responds.

"An hour? It feels like you've been working on that all day," one of the boys states.

I giggle at the way they busted him. He shakes his head and turns toward his car after telling me he's getting the food.

As he walks back he's carrying a mini ice chest. When he's within a few feet, he places it on the floor and opens it up, grabbing a few plates from inside and handing them to me.

"Dinner for you. My mom said, next year, you have to come over in person," he says as I take them from him.

"That's very sweet of her. Let me go place it inside."

When I get to my kitchen, I take a peek and see a full ham dinner with all the side dishes, and on the other plate are slices of both berry pie and apple pie. My mouth waters from the sight of it, but I cover it up and put it in the fridge before I head back outside.

Day One

Once I'm out front again, Drew smiles big. "Okay, now, you have to find the eggs I hid for you."

"You did not."

"It's Easter. Of course I did!"

I grin as I start to search. "Are you going to give me hints?" I ask. "Like, tell me if I'm hot or cold?"

He chuckles under his breath. "Nope. You're on your own on this one."

I let out a huff, totally kidding, and then go back to searching.

I find a few plastic eggs in the flowers and then some in the plants I have on the side of the yard. When I peek in between my front stoop and plants, I see a bright orange bag.

I look up to him and then back to the bag that I know wasn't there before. "Is that an egg? I mean, is that something you put there, or should I be afraid someone hid their dog poop on my porch?"

"Dog poop?" he asks with his head tilted down like, *Are you serious right now?*

"Hey, you never know what people will do nowadays," I say with my hands up in defense.

"Then, no, it's not dog poop. Pick it up."

I do and see it's a San Francisco Giants bag. I reach in and pull out a jersey. Immediately, I drop the bag to the floor and hold up the jersey, flipping it around and squealing when I see *24* written across the back with *MILLER* on the top of it.

I pull it into me. "Do I get to keep it?" I ask with the biggest smile across my face.

He laughs. "Yes. That one's all yours."

I open the buttons and slide it on over my shirt. Once I have the buttons closed again, I spin around to show it off. "How do I look?"

"Amazing," he says with a huge grin.

I blow him a kiss. "Thank you so much. I'd jump on you with a huge hug if I could. I've never worn a jersey, especially with a hunk's name on my back," I say playfully.

He laughs. "The Miller name's never looked so good on someone."

I literally swoon, right there, wanting to fall into a puddle at his feet. After a beat, I inhale, regaining my wits, and ask him, "Stay for dinner?"

A smirk covers his face. "What do you plan on having?"

"I slaved over this ham dinner. I only have a little though, and I'm not sharing, so you'll have to stay a few feet away and sit there and watch me eat, but I swear it will still be fun."

"Probably the most fun I've had in weeks. Count me in."

I turn with an extra giddyup in my step and run into my house to heat up the food his mom plated for me. I stop in the mirror to check out my new jersey. I've never been so proud to wear something in my life.

Day 18

April 13

I flip the bottle I ordered online in my hands, wondering if I'm brave enough to actually do it. This black mask says it does amazing things for your skin and cleans out your pores, but I've heard it's a little difficult to get off.

An idea pops into my head, and I pick up my phone, dialing Drew.

"There's my favorite girl," he says as he answers.

"Whatcha doing?" I singsong.

"Nothing," he singsongs back. "But I have a feeling you have something up your sleeve."

"See, that's why this is going to work between us. You already get me," I say with a huge grin on my face.

"Well, that depends. What are you trying to get me into?"

"I was about to do a black facial mask and thought it would be fun if we did it together."

"A black facial mask? Is this what it's going to be like, living with you? You'll get me to put on avocado masks and paint your toenails when I'm not on the road?"

"Yeah, pretty much. Look at it as our bonding time."

"True, and I guess it's good for my skin with all the dirt and sweat that's normally on it. So, yeah, I'm in. What do I need to get?"

"Come over, and we can stand outside to put it on. Then, you can drive home because it needs to sit for twenty to thirty minutes."

"Let me get this straight. You want me to drive to your house, put something—which I assume, by the name of it, is black—all over my face while standing in your front yard for everyone to see, and then drive back to my place with it still on my face?"

"Uh-huh!"

"Okay, just making sure I had it straight. On my way."

"Bye!" I singsong with a laugh.

When he pulls up, I'm sitting on my porch. I see he's clean-shaven and grin even bigger. Now, he's going to get the full effect.

"Okay, what's this mask I'm putting on my face?" he asks as he approaches me.

It's getting harder and harder not to wrap my arms around him and really say hello. Instead, I throw the bottle his way.

He looks it over and then turns his attention back to me. "Am I going to regret this?" he asks.

"Probably." I grin. "That's why we're going to do it together. Just make sure to not get it near your eyebrows or hairline."

"So, it's a good thing I shaved today?" He rubs his chin.

I nod. "Very. Now, you can get your entire face."

He takes a deep inhale and opens the lid. "Here goes nothing."

He squirts some on his hand, and I hold up the mirror, so he can see what he's doing.

"It's really thick," he says as he rubs it around.

Day One

I try not to giggle at the way he looks with black goo smeared all over his face.

When he's finished, he smiles at me. "How do I look?"

"Like the best boyfriend ever. Here." I hand him a clean towel to wipe his hands off.

"Your turn." He picks up the tube and tosses it to me.

I squeeze it on my fingers and rub it around as he holds up the mirror with the towel covering his hand. Once my face is covered, I stand up straight and smile at him as I clean my hands.

"We're so cute." I reach for my phone. "Here, we have to take a picture."

"You do realize this is the first picture we've taken together, right?"

I smile even bigger. "Then, it's even more perfect."

I turn around and take a selfie of the two of us with our faces covered.

"You have to text that to me," he says. "I can already feel this thing starting to harden. I'll call you when I get back to my place, and you can give me the instructions on how to wash this off."

I raise my eyebrows and try to innocently look off to the side while rocking on my feet.

He eyes me suspiciously. "Is this the part I'm going to regret?"

I hold up the picture, showing him how cute we are together in it. "It will make great memories for sure."

He shakes his head and walks back to his car, turning to point to me before he slides into the driver's seat. "You owe me for this."

"I'll make it worth your while as soon as we're off this quarantine."

He stops and stares at me, his eyes turning darker. I blow him a kiss and run back inside.

A few minutes later, he calls, and I can hear his mom in the background.

"You hear that?" he asks me. "Yeah, that's my mom laughing at me. Apparently, she's well aware of what these so-called black masks are."

I try to hide my giggle. "We're creating memories, remember?"

"And meeting under the quarantine isn't enough?" He chuckles under his breath. "I feel like I can't move my face."

"Only a few more minutes. We're almost there."

"Yeah, but now, I'm more afraid to take it off."

I hear him walk into a room and shut the door.

"Does your mom think I'm crazy?" I ask.

"She thinks I have it bad for you for me to be willing to do such a thing."

His response makes my heart soar. I love how open he is with his feelings. There's no guessing on what's going on or where we stand. It's refreshing.

"What's going to happen when everything's back to normal?" I ask.

"With what?"

"With us?"

"Well, we'll finally be able to have sex, which I can't tell you how bad I've been looking forward to that …"

My face flushes with heat at the thought, and through the mask, it feels even weirder.

"Besides that." I try raising my eyebrows but my face keeps me from doing so.

"Maybe it's best we met this way. We'll already be used to the long-distance thing. I'm not going to lie; I'll be gone a lot. But then, in the off-season, I'll be around a lot, and you'll probably get sick of me."

"Never."

"Ah, you say that now."

Day One

"Just keep doing silly things, like putting on face masks with me, and I'll never get sick of you."

"Deal. Now, can we take this thing off yet?"

I place the call on speakerphone and put the phone down on my counter in the bathroom. I inhale a deep breath. "Okay, let's do this."

He switches his call to speakerphone, too, and when I hear him grunt, I try not to laugh.

"Actually, I lied. I'll never do this again," he says.

"Oh, come on, baby," I taunt.

"Have you even started?"

I stare into the mirror, too afraid to try it yet.

"Come on. You have to remove it sooner or later," he singsongs, making me regret ever doing this to him.

"Okay, on three, we both pull really hard. Ready?"

He sighs into the phone. "You're lucky I like you."

"I know. Okay, one, two ..."

"Three," he says when I don't continue.

He rips his off, and I only make it a few centimeters. I hear him yell as he makes his way around his face, grunting and growling.

"Oh my God! Fuck! Ah, it's ... almost ... okay, and it's off!" His voice is full of relief. "Fuck me, that was painful. How far did you make it?"

I bite my lip. "Not far. I can't. I can't do it. It's like waxing. I can get things waxed, but I can't do it myself."

"Oh, yes, let's talk about that. What exactly do you wax?"

"Drew!" I stomp my feet in frustration. "I'm scared!"

"Come on, Sharee. You got this. I know you can do it."

I slowly peel the mask, and the pain is unreal.

"You have to just rip it off, like a Band-Aid," Drew says.

"Yeah, this is why I don't wear Band-Aids!"

He chuckles under his breath. "Do your best. I'm on my way."

I press the End Call button and continue to try to torture myself by removing a centimeter at a time. Why I ever thought this was a good idea is beyond me.

I step outside when Drew says he's here. As he gets out of his car, he's wearing a cloth mask over his face, which is, of course, made with San Francisco Giants fabric.

"How far did you make it?" he asks.

I lift my chin to show him where only a tiny bit has been pulled off.

"Come here," he says in a calming manner, motioning for me to join him on the sidewalk.

When I stand at his feet, I glance up at him with sadness written all over my face. "Help me," I beg, trying to frown but the mask won't let me.

His hands reach up to my face, and before he goes for the mask, he takes the time to brush my hair out of my face, and then he cups my cheek. I lean into his touch, loving the way it feels against my skin, even with the mask between us.

I look up into his eyes, and my breath hitches. I've never been so close that I can see his eyes like this. The gold flakes shine in the bright sky, and I instantly feel secure with him near.

He takes a shaky breath and then rubs his lips together. "Are you ready?"

I nod. It's going to hurt like hell, but with him doing it, I know I can make it through. Right now, I feel like I can do anything as long as he's next to me.

I lift my hands and place them on his biceps. I feel the goose bumps my touch causes him, and they then cover my flesh as well.

I bite my lower lip as he says, "Okay, here we go."

He pulls the mask, and I flinch, gripping him tighter. Before I know it, my cheek is cleared of the mask.

"Are you doing all right?" he asks.

Day One

I look up into his eyes again and nod. *I'm doing just fine right here.*

He continues to yank it off all the way until it's completely gone. I close my eyes, letting the pain subside as I inhale a deep breath. When I look back into his eyes, I'm instantly lost.

He rubs his finger down my cheek, moving his hand around to the nape of my neck. We stare into each other's eyes, both wanting so much more than we can have right now.

He closes his eyes, takes a deep inhale, and steps back. "Sorry. I should go."

I rub my lips together and nod. My heart pounds as he gets back in his car.

I'm not sure how much longer we can play this game. I've never wanted someone so bad, and the slow torture of not being able to have him is starting to kill me.

Day 19

April 14
Drew

Even though I just woke up and I'm still lying in bed, I pick up the phone to call Sharee.

"Morning," she says when she answers.

My brows furrow when I hear her voice because it's obvious she's not as chipper as normal. "Morning. Did you just wake up?"

"No. I've been up for a while." She sighs. "Just having a bit of a rough time."

I sit up. "Tell me about it."

"It's just …" Her voice cracks, and she takes in a shaky breath. "I think this whole thing has finally gotten to me, you know?"

Now, it's my turn to sigh. "Yeah, I know. Tell me what's going on in that head of yours."

"Technically, we're on spring break, and even though I'm not supposed to be answering emails, a parent reached out to me on Facebook, desperate for an answer. It broke my heart, is all. Her son's been doing his math lessons wrong this entire time, and since they weren't being turned in and graded, he didn't know any different and thought he was doing it right, so he never asked for help.

"This kid is really smart, and he was doing the math correctly, just missing a step to solve the geometry we're focused on now. He did probably three chapters of math wrong. If he's doing it wrong—one of my kids who's really good at math—then what's going on with the kids who aren't good at math?"

I hear her sniff through her nose, and it hurts my heart. To see a teacher care this much about her students is pretty amazing.

"So, what did you say?"

"It's all so confusing. We're asking these kids to do this work and asking their parents to become their teachers, but for what? None of it will be turned in. My principal told me I wouldn't actually be grading anything."

"Then, how will you grade the last semester?"

"It's basically a participation check. Are they checking in? Are they participating in our Zoom lessons? After talking to the parent, we decided that he'll watch videos I found that go over the work, and if he can demonstrate that he understands the chapter by solving a few problems, then he can just move on. I worry about the kids who don't have caring parents like this one does."

I hear more tears fall, and my heart breaks for her. I wish I could go over there and hold her, help her through this time.

"Then, I realized that I'll never see these kids again," she continues. "I love teaching sixth grade because we get to do so many fun things at the end of the year. These kids won't get to go to sixth-grade camp. They won't get to walk the stage at graduation. They won't even get to go tour the junior high, like the students normally do every year." She can barely talk at the end of her sentence because she's crying so much.

"You're an amazing teacher," I say. "I hope you know that."

"Thanks," she says through more tears.

"Please don't cry. I know this is hard for you. I wish I could be there."

"I know." She takes a big inhale before slowly letting it out. "Hey, I have another teacher beeping in. Let me call you back."

"Okay. Call me when you're done. I'll be here."

"I will. Thank you."

I hang up the phone and place it on my bed. I've never felt so helpless, and I hate it.

I get up, throw on some shorts, and head out to the kitchen to get some coffee.

As I sit at the counter, my mom enters the room, pouring herself a cup. "How's my boy this morning?"

I sigh. "I just got off the phone with Sharee. She's having a hard time. A kid did all of his math wrong, and she's heartbroken that she can't be there for him and the rest of her students and for all the end-of-the-year stuff they're going to miss."

"Well, that's a sign of a good teacher. She obviously cares for these kids if it's affecting her that way."

"Yeah, I said the same thing." I stare into my cup.

"Then, why are you so down?"

"Just makes me sad that I can't be there for her."

"You like this girl, don't you?"

I nod. "I really do. I know I just met her, but there's something about her. You know?"

"Of course I know. I wondered if you'd find someone like her. I knew the girls you'd mentioned in the past weren't for you."

Day One

"She's different," I say, playing with my coffee cup.

My mom places her hand over mine. "Then, go to her."

My head pops up to meet her eyes. "What?"

"Go to her. You've done a lot for your dad and me. We'll still need your help, but there's no reason you can't leave things on our doorstep like you've been doing for her. Maybe it's time the roles were reversed."

I look up and see the content on my mom's face. "But, Mom ..."

"No *buts*. I'll be fine. I'll miss seeing your face every day, but I know if all of this wasn't going on, you would have already moved to the city. I'm grateful for the time I've had with you. Now, it's your turn to be with her. Once all of this is over, you'll be on the road again. Maybe even before we're out of lockdown. I don't want you guys to not have your time together. I won't be selfish and keep you all to myself."

I smile and cover her hand with mine. "Thanks, Mom."

The expression on her face says it all. She loves me and wants me to be happy. I finally have the career I've always wanted, and now, I'll have the girl too.

She tilts her head toward the door. "Go get her. But ... maybe shower first." She grins.

I stand up and give her a hug—the last one I'll give her until our lockdown is lifted.

After I shower and get ready as fast as possible, I hop in my car. When I pull out of the driveway, I see my mom and dad standing with their arms around each other, waving good-bye.

Knowing I'm going toward a relationship like the one they've had for years fills me with even more hope.

When I pull up to Sharee's house, I race out of the car, not wanting to waste a second longer. I didn't tell her I was heading over, so I know she's not expecting what's about to come.

I knock on her door and stand with my hands on the frame. Every time I've knocked before, I've stepped back, giving both of us space, but not anymore.

She opens the door, still wearing her PJs with her hair up in a messy bun and a stunned expression on her face.

"Drew," she says breathlessly.

I step into her house and reach out to her, placing my hands on her face and bringing her lips to mine.

She lets out a tiny squeal before throwing her arms around my neck as she falls into our kiss. Our lips mold together, and I pull her closer. As our tongues meet and I taste her for the first time, I let out a growl, only wanting more.

When I move my hands down, she jumps into my arms, wrapping her legs around my waist.

"I couldn't wait any longer," I say between our kisses.

"Thank God!" she yells out.

I laugh as she takes my face in her hands, smiling brightly before leaning in to kiss me again.

I break our kiss, and before I can even ask, she points. "That way."

I smirk. "Yes, ma'am."

Our lips meet again as I walk us to her bedroom. Instead of throwing her down on the bed, I sit and keep her on my lap. She adjusts her legs around my waist, keeping her fingers on my face as our lips explore each other for the first time.

"I'm trying to go slow," I say, kissing her between each word.

"Fuck slow. It's already been slow enough," she says, and I laugh against her neck.

"Well, in that case." I toss her to the side, laying her on the bed.

She giggles, and I slide on top of her, brushing her hair out of her face.

Day One

"I'm pretty sure I'm in love with you," I say as I stare into her eyes.

Her hand reaches up to cup my face. "I love you too, Drew."

I grin. "It's a damn good thing because I'm kind of homeless now." I chuckle.

Her arms wrap around my neck. "You mean, I get you full-time?" she asks with a huge smile.

"You okay with that?"

"Abso-fucking-lutely!" she announces as she leans up and attacks me with her lips.

I run my fingers down her side and lift her shirt up over her head. The fact that she doesn't have a bra on makes my dick even harder than it already is. My hand cups one breast as I slide in between her legs.

"Please tell me this whole no-bra thing is a habit of yours?"

She giggles as her legs wrap around me tighter. "Currently, yes."

"I'm going to love being quarantined with you," I say, leaving kisses down her neck until I get to her breast and suck the tiny bud into my mouth.

Her chest lifts off the bed as her head falls back. I take advantage of her doing so by moving my hand even lower and gliding my fingers below her waistband.

As I slide her pants down her legs, her hands yank my shirt over my head. I assist in the removal of my shirt, and she tosses it to the floor. After I completely remove her pants, I lean in, licking her center through the black lace panties she's wearing.

When I glance up at her, her eyes are closed, and her lips are parted. She's never looked sexier. When her eyes meet mine, she places her hand on my face, and I lean in to her again.

I knew she was different, special, and in this moment,

I feel it even more. This is way more than sex; this here is the rest of my life.

I kiss her stomach and then her thigh as I slide her panties down until they're all the way off. When I lean down and lick her slit, the sound that escapes her lips is fucking perfect. Knowing I made her make that noise is even better.

I want to hear her. I want to hear everything I do to her and never forget it.

"Oh my God!" she screams as her hands dig into my hair and tugs hard.

I shake my head and twirl my tongue more, pressing into her center and devouring the taste I'll never get enough of.

When I pull away, I kiss my way up her body as she greedily yanks at my shorts, trying to push them off with both her hands and feet.

"Wait, I need my wallet to get a condom." I turn toward the floor.

She places her finger under my chin. "I'm on the pill, and you'll be the first guy I've never used protection with. So ..." She leaves the question hanging in the air.

I position my naked body between hers and hold myself on my elbows on either side of her face. Slowly, I kiss her lips. "I've also never *not* used protection. I'm glad you'll be my first."

She nods her head, and I press forward, sliding inside her. She moans, and I drop my forehead to hers. The heat and wetness I feel as she squeezes around me takes my breath away.

Fucking amazing doesn't even begin to cover it.

I look into her eyes as I slide back out and push back in, building a rhythm as we move as one.

As her legs wrap around me tighter, I push harder.

When her fingers scrape down my back in ecstasy, I

growl like I never have before.

I don't want this to stop.

I want to be inside her, right here, for the rest of my life.

This is my home, where I belong and where I'll forever be.

Urgency grows in her moans as her body starts to rock more. When I pick up the pace, her breathing starts to labor.

As her grip on my back tightens, I feel her body start to quiver.

When her screams get louder, I push even harder.

When nothing comes out of her mouth and her entire body goes rigid, I thrust against her and hold her as tight as possible, feeling the waves of her orgasm throughout my entire body as she pulses against my cock.

Her breathing stops, and her arms fall to the sides.

As she comes to again, her eyes open and meet mine. My face, I'm sure, is covered in the biggest smile I've ever had.

Her hands reach up to grip my cheeks as I pound into her, finding my release in seconds. As I start to come, her lips press to mine, and I grunt out as her tongue sweeps into my mouth.

My head falls to her shoulder.

My body is suddenly mush, as the most intense release I've ever felt rushed through my body.

I knew it'd be good with Sharee, but I honestly had no idea it could ever feel like that.

Our breathing is ragged as we both take in what just happened.

When our eyes meet, she grins at me, running her fingers through my hair.

"It's nice to finally get to touch you," she says.

I laugh. "That was a little more than just touching."

"Yeah, well, it sounded better than saying, *It's nice to finally fuck you*," she teases.

"Well, I'd say, the last one will always sound better."

I kiss her lips before falling to my back and pulling her into me. "Do we get to spend every day like this until this shelter in place is over?"

Her fingers run up my chest. "All of a sudden, this shelter-in-place order is the best idea ever!"

I hold her and kiss her forehead. "I couldn't agree more now that I have you by my side."

Epilogue

December 23, 2020
Sharee

I thrust open the front door, carrying more bags than I should. "You'll never believe what I found!" I announce.

Drew comes around the corner from the kitchen, wearing his favorite apron that he wears every time he cooks. Ever since the baseball season ended, he's been working on his cooking skills. He leaves our kitchen in an absolute mess, but the food is amazing, so I don't complain.

"What'd you find?" he asks.

I turn to the Christmas tree sitting in the corner and place the bags on the floor next to it. When I face him, his expression tells me something's up. I pause, searching around our home.

Drew pretty much never left my place after the day we finally broke the no-touching rule. To go from barely knowing someone to living with them twenty-four/seven should have been scary, but it wasn't one bit.

We had more fun than I'd ever had with anyone else. He let me give him manicures, and then he'd paint my toenails. We'd lie around in bed all morning and exercise all afternoon. It was the perfect blend of our time.

He taught me how to properly throw a ball and hit off a T, and he kept reminding me that I needed to show up all the other WAGs out there. I took my new role very seriously, and I even ordered gear online, so I'd look the baseball part as well.

When Drew put the eye black under my eyes, it was official that I was the best baseball WAG there'd ever been. We took pictures of us, and when it was time to send out our Christmas cards, there was no question those were the pictures to send.

The quarantine was hard on everyone, and I'm sure it's even something people would rather forget ever took place but not us. It's such a big part of our story and one that we'll celebrate as a piece of our history together.

It was rough when the baseball season started back up and he went on the road, but we were used to being apart, so we acted like we were back on the shelter-in-place order again. Re-creating our phone sex with different books was my favorite part.

And you can bet, when he played in San Francisco, I was right there, cheering him on at every game, until school started again.

Going back to school felt weird since we'd never really finished the previous year. I had an entirely new group of kids, who I've grown to love just as much, but my students from last year will always hold a special place in my heart.

"Why are you looking at me like that?" I ask, and Drew's smirk grows. "What?"

He shrugs but can't play off the grin that's spreading on his face by the second.

I search around the area. "What did you do?"

"Now, why do you think I did anything?" He tilts his head, and it's a dead giveaway. The guy can't lie for shit.

Day One

"You're up to something. Tell me." I step toward him.

"You'll have to find it for yourself."

I narrow my eyes at him. "Are you going to give me a hint?"

He shakes his head and acts like he's zipping his lips shut and throwing away the key.

I look over his shoulder. "What are you cooking?"

"I'm making that chicken pasta meal we made the first time we cooked together."

"Aw, the one we made over the phone?"

"That's the one!" He smiles big but then glances around the room again.

"But that's not why your face looks like that," I accuse.

"Looks like what?" he says with a laugh.

I slowly make my way past him, searching for something that's out of place. He's made a huge mess in the kitchen with his one-pot meal, but that's normal, so it's not what's making him act so weird.

When I turn around, he's still standing in the middle of our living room, proving that, yes, something is definitely up with him.

"Drew!" I whine playfully.

"Sharee!" He copies my tone.

I give him the evil eye as I walk back into the living room.

That's when I see it. Something's hidden in the tree.

My breath hitches as I stare at the tiny black box resting on a branch right at eye-level. I look at him, and he tilts his head toward the box with a grin on his face.

I run to it, grabbing it so fast I almost knock over other decorations. Rubbing my lips together, I close my eyes and mentally prepare for what this means.

I knew Drew and I were perfect together, but we haven't really talked about marriage. Of course, I wanted to talk about it, but I didn't want to rush things. Our entire relationship had been rushed, so I figured it would come when he was ready. Knowing he's ready without us even talking about it is beyond a dream come true.

If there's one thing I know without a doubt, it's that he loves me, and we have forever to make things official, so I haven't been in a hurry to bring it up.

When I turn to face him, I see that he's moved closer.

He grins when he says, "Open it."

I take a deep inhale and slowly open the lid to the velvet box. When I see what's inside, I pause and squint my eyes. Lifting the gold string, I hold it up closer to see what it is.

A flat wooden Christmas ornament of toilet paper reads, *I love you more than toilet paper—2020.*

I laugh out loud and hold it up for him. "Are you serious right now?"

"What?" He steps closer. "I thought it was perfect for us. Our first ornament together."

I look into his eyes, and he's right. It's the perfect ornament, and it tells our story together in only a way it could.

I rise to my tippy toes to kiss him. "That's sweet. Thank you."

"You don't like it?" he asks.

"No, I love it. Look, I'm going to place it right here, so when everyone comes over, it'll be the first ornament they see."

I hang it on the tree, and when I flip around again to face him, he's on one knee, holding up a diamond ring.

"Were you expecting this instead?"

My hands instantly cover my mouth as a squeal escapes my lips.

"Sharee?"

I jump into his arms. "Yes, yes, yes, Drew!" I cheer.

He laughs. "But I haven't asked you anything yet."

"Oh, yeah, sorry." I wrap my arms around his neck,

staying on his lap. "Continue." I try to act as serious as possible.

He softly kisses my lips, and then he takes a deep breath before trying again. "You came into my life in the most uncertain time, yet everything about you was filled with certainty. You made dark times bright, and you have filled my life with everything I thought was missing. Seeing you at my games with my jersey on, your hair in pigtails, and more orange than the fruit itself covering your entire body made me proud to call you mine. I want to see if you'll make Miller your last name, too, so the jersey is as true as it can possibly be. Sharee, will you marry me?"

"Yes, yes, yes!" I scream and lean in to kiss him.

"It's okay if you need to think about it a little," he says through his chuckles.

"Oh, stop. I'm going to be the best WAG now because everyone knows the wives mean the most, and everyone will know I'm yours."

He pulls back to look me in the eyes. "Of that, I have no doubt!"

July 14, 2021

Drew was voted to be on the MLB All-Star team, and this week has been a whirlwind of events, parties, and more. Seeing him living his dream is the best part of being his wife.

We were married in a small wedding on March 27, a year to the day from when he messaged me on Tinder. Yes, it was during spring training, but the day meant more to us than having some big event.

Our wedding was perfect for us with only our families and a few close friends in attendance. And, yes, we had toilet paper rolls lining the aisle as I headed toward the most amazing man I'd ever met, waiting there to make me his wife.

I have one more surprise for him, and I figure being here, where he's living his dream, is the best place to tell him.

The store at the stadium sells jerseys of every player, and while he's warming up, I make my way there to buy exactly what I'm looking for.

We have a ritual where, before every game starts, he comes up to me in the stands and leans through the net to give me a kiss. It makes it interesting to kiss through the nets, but we don't care.

We've been covered on pretty much every news station, and we've had more fans ooh and aah than I can remember. It's my favorite part of being in his life.

As he heads toward me, I reach for my bag and hold up what I bought.

I watch as what I'm doing computes in his head. I take the tiny jersey that says *Miller #24* across the back and place it to my stomach. That's when it hits him.

His eyes widen, and a huge smile grows across his face as he runs the remainder of the way to me. "Is this what I think?" he asks, his face completely lit up.

I nod with the same grin on my face.

He kisses me through the net before turning and racing to where there's no more fencing keeping him out of the stands. He jumps the small barrier, and I laugh at his antics before making my way toward him.

He squeezes past all the fans who are in shock to see him walking through the stands, having no clue what's going on.

Fans reach out to pat him on the back as I hear him saying, "Excuse me. Sorry. I just need to get through."

When he finally reaches me, I'm laughing so hard. He

doesn't care when he picks me up and kisses me with everyone around.

When he places me down, he takes the jersey, holding it up in the air for everyone to see, and screams, "We're having a baby!"

The crowd erupts in cheers and clapping. Tears fall down my face as I take in his reaction. I knew he'd be happy, but I had no idea he'd be this elated.

Just like the quarantine surprised us all, Drew continues to surprise me in the most amazing way. We definitely took a bad situation and made the best of it, and now, we'll have our own little reminder of the time in our world that no one will ever forget.

Acknowledgments

I had an idea a few days into the Shelter-in-Place orders set forth by our Government here in California during the COVID-19 national crisis ... A chapter a night posted to Facebook, written in live time about a couple who met during the quarantine via Tinder. I had no idea how long it would last or if people would even follow along.

It turned into so much more than I ever imagined. Getting to interact with the readers everyday was the main thing to get me by on those days where I just wanted my normal life back.

I had a lot of requests to release this as a full book so if you enjoyed this thank those readers on Facebook for pushing me to continue. I was sad when their story ended, but after writing a chapter a day for 19 straight days I felt their story was told.

Thank you everyone who followed along with Drew and Sharee's adventure. I can't tell you what your support has meant to me over these past few weeks.

Thank you again for joining me on this journey. Take care everyone, and stay healthy out there!

About the Author

Lauren Runow is the author of multiple Adult Contemporary Romance novels, some more dirty than others. When Lauren isn't writing, you'll find her listening to music, at her local CrossFit, reading, or at the baseball field with her boys. Her only vice is coffee, and she swears it makes her a better mom!

Lauren is a graduate from the Academy of Art in San Francisco and is the founder and co-owner of the community magazine she and her husband publish. She is a proud Rotarian, helps run a local non-profit kids science museum, and was awarded Woman of the Year from Congressman Garamendi. She lives in Northern California with her husband and two sons.

You can also stay in touch through the social media links below.

Sign up for her newsletter at http://bit.ly/2NEXgH1

Check out her books on Goodreads: http://bit.ly/1Isw3Sv

Follow her on:
Facebook at https://www.facebook.com/laurenjrunow
Instagram at https://instagram.com/Lauren_Runow/
BookBub at https://www.bookbub.com/authors/lauren-runow
Twitter at https://twitter.com/LaurenRunow
BookandMain: https://bookandmainbites.com/LaurenRunow

Join her reader group on Facebook:
Lauren's Law Breakers

You can also visit her website at www.laurenrunow.com or email her at lauren@laurenrunow.com.